Jane Eyre

by Charlotte Bronte

Annotated and Abridged

The Best Dialogue and Narrative Parts

Edited by

Paul and Brenda Neal

Introduction

Jane Eyre – Annotated and Abridged – The Best Dialogue and Narrative Parts is a highly edited version of the story. *Jane Eyre* is one of the most popular novels of all time. The delight of this story is the tension and sparring between the governess Jane Eyre and her master Mr. Rochester, a guarded then passionate meeting of minds and hearts. The dialogue between these two main characters is the thrust of the book. Some pithy narrative is included in addition to dialogue.

Editing is very subjective. The language of *Jane Eyre, nine*teenth century British English, has an elegance and an intriguing timeless resonance. Of course some parts of the story are more compelling than other parts. We have chosen to focus mainly on the sparky synergy between these two feisty characters. Some subplots are covered in a sentence or two.

Jane Eyre in its entirety is a masterpiece. However, for the reader who wants to admire the jewels, it can be argued that this edited version has a place.

How could anyone dare to edit what is considered to be one of the best books ever written?

We of the 21st Century have a shorter attention span. We are used to reading a lot online that is reduced to bullet points. Far better to read some *Jane Eyre* than none of it.

And regarding shortening and altering original manuscripts, movies adapt and compress literary works, relying mostly on dialogue and often taking great artistic liberties. Also graphic novels edit and abridge classic literature. And, we had a personal demonstration of the power and attraction of dialogue. Our granddaughter from the age of three on would repeatedly reenact pivotal dialogue scenes from *Cinderella, The Little Mermaid, Frozen,* and other stories.

Jane Eyre has mystery, suspense, a horrendous secret, tragedy, class distinctions, a Gothic mansion, high society hobnobbing, love rivalry, snobbery, snide and catty remarks, humor, propriety, restraint, confessions, and more.

We have set off our added brief condensed narrative for the plot movement with brackets – [[   ]].

We have changed some British spellings to American spellings. We have changed some obscure wording and streamlined. We have included more paragraph breaks to ease reading.

Paul and Brenda Neal

Jane Eyre is a Public Domain work.

Online there are several links to read *Jane Eyre* for free.

[[Jane Eyre was an oppressed, orphaned child. She lived with an aunt and hostile taunting cousins. Her aunt rejected her, treated her abominably, and punished her cruelly. The aunt sent her to boarding school. Her early years there were an experience of continued deprivation and suffering. Jane lost her best friend to typhoid. Circumstances improved and Jane stayed at the boarding school for a few years and taught there for two years. Then to expand her horizons she accepted a job as a governess at Thornfield Manor to a French child, Adele.]]

[[Jane's employer, the guardian of the French child, was a dark edgy brusque man, Edward Rochester. Jane first met him when his horse slipped on ice causing him to fall. Jane offered assistance. Mr. Rochester did not identify himself as the master of Thornfield Manor.]]

[[Jane first officially met Mr. Rochester with her student Adele and Mrs. Fairfax the housekeeper. Despite his aloof cynical manner Jane found herself attracted to him.]]

As he took the cup from my hand, Adele, thinking the moment propitious for making a request in my favor, cried out—

"N'est-ce pas, monsieur, qu'il y a un cadeau pour Mademoiselle Eyre dans votre petit coffre?"

"Who talks of cadeaux?" said he gruffly. "Did you expect a present, Miss Eyre? Are you fond of presents?" and he searched my face with eyes that I saw were dark, irate, and piercing.

"I hardly know, sir; I have little experience of them: they are generally thought pleasant things."

"Generally thought? But what do YOU think?"

"I should be obliged to take time, sir, before I could give you an answer worthy of your acceptance: a present has many faces to it, has it not? and one should consider all, before pronouncing an opinion as to its nature."

"Miss Eyre, you are not so unsophisticated as Adele: she demands a 'cadeau,' clamorously, the moment she sees me: you beat about the bush."

"Because I have less confidence in my deserts than Adele has: she can prefer the claim of old acquaintance, and the right too of custom; for she says you have always been in the habit of giving her playthings; but if I had to make out a case I should be puzzled, since I am a stranger, and have done nothing to entitle me to an acknowledgment."

"Oh, don't fall back on over modesty! I have examined Adele, and find you have taken great pains with her: she is not bright, she has no talents; yet in a short time she has made much improvement."

"Sir, you have now given me my 'cadeau;' I am obliged to you: it is the meed teachers most covet—praise of their pupils' progress."

Mr. Rochester took his tea in silence.

"Come to the fire," said the master, when the tray was taken away, and Mrs. Fairfax had settled into a corner with her knitting; while Adele was leading me by the hand round the room, showing me beautiful books and ornaments.

"You have been resident in my house three months?"

"Yes, sir."

"And you came from—?"

"From Lowood school, in—shire."

"Ah! a charitable concern. How long were you there?"

"Eight years."

"Eight years! you must be tenacious of life. No wonder you have rather the look of another world. I marveled where you had got that sort of face. When you came on me in Hay Lane last night, I thought unaccountably of fairy tales, and had half a mind to demand whether you had bewitched my horse: I am not sure yet. Who are your parents?"

"I have none."

"Nor ever had, I suppose: do you remember them?"

"No."

"I thought not. And so you were waiting for your people when my horse slipped on the ice and I fell?"

"For whom, sir?"

"For the men in green: it was a proper moonlight evening for them. Did I break through one of your rings, that you spread that damned ice on the causeway?"

I shook my head. "The men in green all forsook England a hundred years ago," said I, speaking as seriously as he had done. "I don't think either summer or harvest, or winter moon, will ever shine on their revels more."

Mrs. Fairfax had dropped her knitting, and, with raised eyebrows, seemed wondering what sort of talk this was.

"Well," resumed Mr. Rochester, "if you disown parents, you must have some sort of kinsfolk: uncles and aunts?"

"No; none that I ever saw."

"And your home?"

"I have none."

"Where do your brothers and sisters live?"

"I have no brothers or sisters."

"Who recommended you to come here?"

"I advertised, and Mrs. Fairfax answered my advertisement."

"Have you read much?"

"Only such books as came in my way; and they have not been numerous or very learned."

"You have lived the life of a nun: no doubt you are well drilled in religious forms;—Brocklehurst, who I understand directs Lowood, is a parson, is he not?"

"I disliked Mr. Brocklehurst; and I was not alone in the feeling. He is a harsh man; at once pompous and meddling; he cut off our hair; and for economy's sake bought us bad needles and thread, with which we could hardly sew."

"And was that the head and front of his offending?" demanded Mr. Rochester.

"He starved us and he bored us with long lectures once a week, and with evening readings about sudden deaths and judgments, which made us afraid to go to bed."

"What age were you when you went to Lowood?"

"About ten."

"And you stayed there eight years: you are now, then, eighteen?"

I assented.

"Arithmetic, you see, is useful; without its aid, I should hardly have been able to guess your age. It is a point difficult to fix where the features and countenance are so much at variance as in your case. And now what did you learn at Lowood? Can you play?"

"A little."

"Of course: that is the established answer. Go into the library—I mean, if you please.—(Excuse my tone of command; I am used to say, "Do this," and it is done: I cannot alter my customary habits for one new inmate.)—Go, then, into the library and play a tune."

I departed, obeying his directions. "Enough!" he called out in a few minutes. "You play A LITTLE, I see; like any other English school girl; perhaps rather better than some, but not well."

I closed the piano and returned. Mr. Rochester continued—"Adele showed me some sketches this morning, which she said were yours. I don't know whether they were entirely of your doing; probably a master aided you?"

"No, indeed!" I interjected.

"Ah! Well, fetch me your portfolio."

I brought the portfolio from the library. He deliberately scrutinized each sketch and painting. Three he laid aside; the others, when he had examined them, he swept from him.

"And when did you find time to do them? They have taken much time, and some thought."

"I did them in the last two vacations I spent at Lowood, when I had no other occupation."

"Where did you get your copies?"

"Out of my head."

"That head I see now on your shoulders?"

"Yes, sir."

"Has it other furniture of the same kind within?"

"I should think it may have: I should hope—better." He spread the pictures before him, and again surveyed them alternately.

"Were you happy when you painted these pictures?" asked Mr. Rochester presently.

"I was absorbed, sir: yes, and I was happy. To paint them, in short, was to enjoy one of the keenest pleasures I have ever known."

"That is not saying much. Your pleasures, by your own account, have been few; but I daresay you did exist in a kind of artist's dreamland while you blended and arranged these strange tints. Did you sit at them long each day?"

"I had nothing else to do, because it was the vacation, and I sat at them from morning till noon, and from noon till night: the length of the midsummer days."

"And you felt self satisfied with the result of your ardent labors?"

"Far from it. I was tormented by the contrast between my idea and my handiwork: in each case I had imagined something which I was quite powerless to realize."

"Not quite: you have secured the shadow of your thought; but no more, probably. You had not enough of the artist skill and science to give it full being: yet the drawings are, for a school girl, peculiar. As to the thoughts, they are elfish. These eyes in the Evening Star you must have seen in a dream. How could you make them look so clear, and yet not at all brilliant? for the planet above quells their rays. And what meaning is that in their solemn depth? And who taught you to paint wind. There is a high gale in that sky, and on this hill top."

I had scarce tied the strings of the portfolio, when, looking at his watch, he said abruptly—

"It is nine o"clock: what are you about, Miss Eyre, to let Adele sit up so long? Take her to bed."

Adele went to kiss him. He endured the caress, but scarcely seemed to relish it.

"I wish you all goodnight, now," said he, making a movement of the hand towards the door, in token that he was tired of our company, and wished to dismiss us. Mrs. Fairfax folded up her knitting: I took my portfolio: we curtseyed to him, received a frigid bow in return, and so withdrew.

[[The next conversation between Jane and Mr. Rochester —]]

"Ah! well, come forward; be seated here." He drew a chair near his own. "I am not fond of the prattle of children," he continued; "for, an old bachelor I am. It would be intolerable to me to pass a whole evening tete-e-tete with a brat. Don't draw that chair farther off, Miss Eyre; sit down exactly where I placed it—if you please, that is. Confound these civilities!

Miss Eyre, draw your chair still a little farther forward: you are yet too far back; I cannot see you without disturbing my position in this comfortable chair, which I have no mind to do."

I did as I was bid, though I would much rather have remained somewhat in the shade; but Mr. Rochester had such a direct way of giving orders, it seemed a matter of course to obey him promptly.

He had been looking two minutes at the fire, and I had been looking the same length of time at him, when, turning suddenly, he caught my gaze.

"You examine me, Miss Eyre," said he: "do you think me handsome?"

I should, if I had deliberated, have replied to this question by something conventionally vague and polite; but the answer somehow slipped from my tongue before I was aware—"No, sir."

"Ah! By my word! there is something singular about you," said he: "you have the air of a little nonnette; quaint, quiet, grave, and simple, as you sit with your hands before you, and your eyes generally bent on the carpet and when one asks you a question, or makes a remark to which you are obliged to reply, you rap out a round rejoinder, which, if not blunt, is at least brusque. What do you mean by it?"

"Sir, I was too plain; I beg your pardon. I ought to have replied that it was not easy to give an impromptu answer to a question about appearances; that tastes mostly differ; and that beauty is of little consequence, or something of that sort."

"You ought to have replied no such thing. Beauty of little consequence, indeed! Go on: what fault do you find with me, pray? I suppose I have all my limbs and all my features like any other man?"

"Mr. Rochester, allow me to disown my first answer: I intended no pointed repartee: it was only a blunder."

"Now, ma"am, am I a fool?"

"Far from it, sir. You would, perhaps, think me rude if I inquired in return whether you are a philanthropist?"

"There again! When she pretended to pat my head: and that is because I said I did not like the society of children and old women. No, young lady, I am not a general philanthropist; but I bear a conscience. And, besides, I once had a kind of rude tenderness of heart. When I was as old as you, I was a feeling fellow enough, partial to the unfledged, unfostered, and unlucky; but Fortune has knocked me about since. Yes: does that leave hope for me?"

"Decidedly he has had too much wine," I thought; and I did not know what answer to make to his queer question.

"You looked very much puzzled, Miss Eyre; and though you are not pretty any more than I am handsome, yet a puzzled air becomes you; besides, it is convenient, for it keeps those searching eyes of yours away from my physiognomy, so puzzle on. Young lady, I am disposed to be gregarious and communicative tonight."

With this announcement he rose from his chair, and stood, leaning his arm on the marble mantelpiece. I am sure most people would have thought him an ugly man; yet there was so much ease in his demeanor; such a look of complete indifference to his own external appearance to atone for the lack of mere personal attractiveness.

"I am disposed to be gregarious and communicative tonight," he repeated, "and that is why I sent for you: the fire and the chandelier were not sufficient company for me; nor would Pilot have been, for none of these can talk. Adele is a degree better, but still far below the mark; Mrs. Fairfax ditto; you, I am persuaded, can suit me if you will: you puzzled me the first evening I invited you down here. I have almost forgotten you since. But tonight I am resolved to be at ease and recall what pleases. It would please me now to draw you out—to learn more of you—therefore speak." Instead of speaking, I smiled; and not a very complacent or submissive smile either.

"Speak," he urged.

"What about, sir?"

"Whatever you like. I leave both the choice of subject and the manner of treating it entirely to yourself."

Accordingly I sat and said nothing: "If he expects me to talk for the mere sake of talking and showing off, he will find he has addressed himself to the wrong person," I thought.

"You are dumb, Miss Eyre." I was dumb still. He bent his head a little towards me, and with a single hasty glance seemed to dive into my eyes. "Stubborn?" he said, "and annoyed. Ah! it is consistent. I put my request in an absurd, almost insolent form. Miss Eyre, I beg your pardon.

"The fact is, once for all, I don't wish to treat you like an inferior. I claim only such superiority as must result from twenty years' difference in age and a century's advance in experience. This is legitimate, and it is by virtue of this superiority, and this alone, that I desire you to have the goodness to talk to me a little now, and divert my thoughts, which are galled with dwelling on one point—cankering as a rusty nail."

He had deigned an explanation, almost an apology, and I did not feel insensible to his condescension, and would not seem so.

"I am willing to amuse you, if I can, sir—quite willing; but I cannot introduce a topic, because how do I know what will interest you? Ask me questions, and I will do my best to answer them."

"Then, in the first place, do you agree with me that I have a right to be a little masterful, abrupt, perhaps exacting, sometimes, on the grounds I stated, namely, that I am old enough to be your father, and that I have battled through a varied experience with many men of many nations, and roamed over half the globe, while you have lived quietly with one set of people in one house?"

"Do as you please, sir."

"That is no answer; or rather it is a very irritating, because a very evasive one. Reply clearly."

"I don't think, sir, you have a right to command me, merely because you are older than I, or because you have seen more of the world than I have; your claim to superiority depends on the use you have made of your time and experience."

"Promptly spoken. But I won"t allow that, seeing that it would never suit my case, as I have made an indifferent, not to say a bad, use of both advantages. Leaving superiority out of the question, then, you must still agree to receive my orders now and then, without being piqued or hurt by the tone of command. Will you?"

I smiled: I thought to myself Mr. Rochester IS peculiar— he seems to forget that he pays me 30 pounds per annum for receiving his orders.

"The smile is very well," said he, catching instantly the passing expression; "but speak too."

"I was thinking, sir, that very few masters would trouble themselves to inquire whether or not their paid subordinates were piqued and hurt by their orders."

"Paid subordinates! What! you are my paid subordinate, are you? Oh yes, I had forgotten the salary! Well then, on that mercenary ground, will you agree to let me hector a little?"

"No, sir, not on that ground; but, on the ground that you did forget it, and that you care whether or not a dependent is comfortable in his dependency, I agree heartily."

"And will you consent to dispense with a great many conventional forms and phrases, without thinking that the omission arises from insolence?"

"I am sure, sir, I should never mistake informality for insolence: one I rather like, the other nothing free born would submit to, even for a salary."

"Humbug! Most things free born will submit to anything for a salary; therefore, keep to yourself, and don't venture on generalities of which you are intensely ignorant. However, I mentally shake hands with you for your answer, despite its inaccuracy; and as much for the manner in which it was said, as for the substance of the speech; the manner was frank and sincere; one does not often see such a manner: no, on the contrary, affectation, or coldness, or stupid, coarse minded misapprehension of one's meaning are the usual rewards of candor.

"Not three in three thousand raw school girl governesses would have answered me as you have just done. But I don't mean to flatter you: if you are cast in a different mold to the majority, it is no merit of yours: Nature did it. And then, after all, I go too fast in my conclusions: for what I yet know, you may be no better than the rest; you may have intolerable defects to counterbalance your few good points."

"And so may you," I thought. My eye met his as the idea crossed my mind: he seemed to read the glance, answering as if its import had been spoken as well as imagined—

"Yes, yes, you are right," said he; "I have plenty of faults of my own: I know it, and I don't wish to palliate them, I assure you. God wot I need not be too severe about others; I have a past existence, a series of deeds, a color of life to contemplate. I like to lay half the blame on ill fortune and adverse circumstances. I was thrust on to a wrong tack at the age of one-and-twenty, and have never recovered the right course since: but I might have been very different; I might have been as good as you— wiser—almost as stainless. I envy you your peace of mind, your clean conscience, your unpolluted memory. Little girl, a memory without blot or contamination must be an exquisite treasure— an inexhaustible source of pure refreshment: is it not?"

"How was your memory when you were eighteen, sir?"

"I was your equal at eighteen quite your equal. Nature meant me to be, on the whole, a good man, Miss Eyre; one of the better kind, and you see I am not so. You would say you don't see it; at least I flatter myself I read as much in your eye. Then take my word for it,—I am not a villain: you are not to suppose that —not to attribute to me any such bad eminence; but, owing, I verily believe, rather to circumstances than to my natural bent, I am a trite commonplace sinner, hackneyed in all the poor petty dissipations with which the rich and worthless try to put on life.

"Do you wonder that I avow this to you? Know, that in the course of your future life you will often find yourself elected the involuntary confidant of your acquaintances' secrets: people will instinctively find out, as I have done, that it is not your forte to tell of yourself, but to listen while others talk of themselves; they will feel, too, that you listen with no malevolent scorn of their indiscretion, but with a kind of innate sympathy; not the less comforting and encouraging because it is very unobtrusive in its manifestations."

"How do you know?—how can you guess all this, sir?"

"I know it well; therefore I proceed almost as freely as if I were writing my thoughts in a diary. You would say, I should have been superior to circumstances; so I should— so I should; but you see I was not. When fate wronged me, I had not the wisdom to remain cool: I turned desperate; then I degenerated. Dread remorse when you are tempted to err, Miss Eyre; remorse is the poison of life."

"Where are you going?

"To put Adele to bed: it is past her bedtime."

"You are afraid of me, because I talk like a Sphynx."

"Your language is enigmatical, sir: but though I am bewildered, I am certainly not afraid."

"You ARE afraid—your self love dreads a blunder."

"In that sense I do feel apprehensive—I have no wish to talk nonsense."

"If you did, it would be in such a grave, quiet manner, I should mistake it for sense. Do you never laugh, Miss Eyre? Don't trouble yourself to answer—I see you laugh rarely; but you can laugh very merrily: believe me, you are not naturally austere, any more than I am naturally vicious. The constraint of your childhood still clings to you somewhat; controlling your features, muffling your voice, and restricting your limbs; and you fear in the presence of a man and a brother— or father, or master, or what you will—to smile too gaily, speak too freely, or move too quickly: but, in time, I think you will learn to be natural with me, as I find it impossible to be conventional with you; and then your looks and movements will have more vivacity and variety than they dare offer now. I see at intervals the glance of a curious sort of bird through the close set bars of a cage: a vivid, restless, resolute captive is there; were it but free, it would soar cloud high. You are still bent on going?"

"It has struck nine, sir."

"Never mind,—wait a minute: Adele is not ready to go to bed yet. My position, Miss Eyre, with my back to the fire, and my face to the room, favors observation. While talking to you, I have also occasionally watched Adele (I have my own reasons for thinking her a curious study,—reasons that I may, nay, that I shall, impart to you some day). She pulled out of her box, about ten minutes ago, a little pink silk frock; rapture lit her face as she unfolded it; coquetry runs in her blood, blends with her brains, and seasons the marrow of her bones. "Il faut que je l'essaie!" cried she, "et e l'instant meme!" and she rushed out of the room. She is now with Sophie, undergoing a robing process: in a few minutes she will re-enter; and I know what I shall see,—a miniature of Celine Varens, as she used to appear on the boards at the rising of— But never mind that."

Mr. Rochester did, on a future occasion, explain it. It was one afternoon, when he chanced to meet me and Adele in the grounds: and while she played with Pilot, he asked me to walk up and down a long beech avenue within sight of her.

He then said that she was the daughter of a French opera dancer, Celine Varens, towards whom he had once cherished what he called a "grande passion." This passion Celine had professed to return with even superior ardor. He thought himself her idol, ugly as he was.

"And, Miss Eyre, so much was I flattered by this preference of the Gallic sylph for her British gnome, that I installed her in an hotel; gave her a complete establishment of servants, a carriage, cashmeres, diamonds, dentelles, etc. In short, I began the process of ruining myself in the received style, like any other spoony.

"I had not, it seems, the originality to chalk out a new road to shame and destruction, but trode the old track with stupid exactness not to deviate an inch from the beaten center I had—as I deserved to have—the fate of all other spoonies. Happening to call one evening when Celine did not expect me, I found her out; but it was a warm night, and I was tired with strolling through Paris, so I sat down in her boudoir; happy to breathe the air consecrated so lately by her presence.

"No,—I exaggerate; I never thought there was any consecrating virtue about her: it was rather a sort of pastille perfume she had left; a scent of musk and amber, than an odor of sanctity. I was just beginning to stifle with the fumes of conservatory flowers and sprinkled essences, when I bethought myself to open the window and step out on to the balcony. It was moonlight and gaslight besides, and very still and serene. I sat down, and took out a cigar,—I will take one now, if you will excuse me."

Here ensued a pause, filled up by the producing and lighting of a cigar; having placed it to his lips and breathed a trail of Havannah incense on the freezing and sunless air, he went on—

"I liked bonbons too in those days, Miss Eyre, and I was croquant— (overlook the barbarism)—croquant chocolate comfits, and smoking alternately, watching meantime the equipages that rolled along the fashionable streets towards the neighboring opera house, when in an elegant close carriage drawn by a beautiful pair of English horses, and distinctly seen in the brilliant city night, I recognized the 'voiture' I had given Celine. She was returning: of course my heart thumped with impatience.

"The carriage stopped, as I had expected, at the hotel door; my flame (that is the very word for an opera inamorata) alighted: though muffed in a cloak—an unnecessary encumbrance on so warm a June evening—I knew her instantly. Bending over the balcony, I was about to murmur "' ange'—in a tone, of course, which should be audible to the ear of love alone—when a figure jumped from the carriage after her.

"You never felt jealousy, did you, Miss Eyre? Of course not: I need not ask you; because you never felt love. You have both sentiments yet to experience: your soul sleeps; the shock is yet to be given which shall waken it. You think all existence lapses in as quiet a flow as that in which your youth has hitherto slid away.

"But I tell you—and you may mark my words—you will come some day to a craggy pass in the channel, where the whole of life's stream will be broken up into whirl and tumult, foam and noise: either you will be dashed to atoms on crag points, or lifted up and borne on by some master wave into a calmer current as I am now.

"I like this day; I like that sky of steel; I like the sternness and stillness of the world under this frost. I like Thornfield, its antiquity, its old crow trees and thorn trees, its grey facade, and lines of dark windows reflecting that metal welkin: and yet how long have I abhorred the very thought of it, shunned it like a great plague house? How I do still abhor—."

He ground his teeth and was silent: he arrested his step and struck his boot against the hard ground. Some hated thought seemed to have him in its grip, and to hold him so tightly that he could not advance.

We were ascending the avenue when he thus paused; the hall was before us. He cast a glare such as I never saw before or since, pain, shame, ire, impatience, disgust, detestation. Wild was the wrestle but another feeling rose and triumphed: something hard and cynical: self willed and resolute: it settled his passion and he went on—

"During the moment I was silent, Miss Eyre, I was arranging a point with my destiny. She stood there, by that beech trunk—a hag like one of those who appeared to Macbeth.

He subjoined moodily, "I wish to be a better man than I have been, than I am."

I ventured to recall him to the point whence he had abruptly diverged—"Did you leave the balcony, sir," I asked, "when Mdlle. Varens entered?"

I almost expected a rebuff for this hardly well timed question, but he turned his eyes towards me.

"Oh, I had forgotten Celine! When I saw my charmer thus come in accompanied by a cavalier, I seemed to hear a hiss, and the green snake of jealousy, rising on undulating coils from the moonlit balcony, glided within me, and ate its way in two minutes to my heart's core.

"Strange!" he exclaimed, suddenly starting again from the point. "Strange that I should choose you for the confidant of all this, young lady; passing strange that you should listen to me quietly, as if it were the most usual thing in the world for a man like me to tell stories of his opera mistresses to a quaint, inexperienced girl like you! But the last singularity explains the first, as I intimated once before: you, with your gravity, considerateness, and caution were made to be the recipient of secrets.

"Besides, I know what sort of a mind I have placed in communication with my own: I know it is one not liable to take infection: it is a peculiar mind: it is a unique one."

"I remained on the balcony. 'They will come to her boudoir, no doubt,' thought I: 'let me prepare an ambush.'"

There was 'the Varens,' shining in satin and jewels,—my gifts of course,— and there was her companion in an officer's uniform; and I knew him for a young roue of a vicomte—a brainless and vicious youth whom I had sometimes met in society, and had never thought of hating because I despised him so absolutely.

"On recognizing him, the fang of the snake Jealousy was instantly broken; because at the same moment my love for Celine sank under an extinguisher. A woman who could betray me for such a rival was not worth contending for; she deserved only scorn; less, however, than I, who had been her dupe.

"They began to talk; their conversation eased me completely: frivolous, mercenary, heartless, and senseless, it was rather calculated to weary than enrage a listener. A card of mine lay on the table; this being perceived, brought my name under discussion. Neither of them possessed energy or wit to belabor me soundly, but they insulted me as coarsely as they could in their little way: especially Celine, who even waxed rather brilliant on my personal defects.

"Now it had been her custom to launch out into fervent admiration of what she called my 'beaute male:' wherein she differed diametrically from you, who told me point blank, at the second interview, that you did not think me handsome. The contrast struck me at the time.

"Opening the window, I walked in upon them; liberated Celine from my protection; gave her notice to vacate her hotel; offered her a purse for immediate exigencies; disregarded screams, hysterics, prayers, protestations, convulsions; made an appointment with the vicomte for a meeting at the Bois de Boulogne. Next morning I had the pleasure of encountering him; left a bullet in one of his arms. And then thought I had done with the whole crew. But unluckily the Varens, six months before, had given me this filette Adele, who, she affirmed, was my daughter; and perhaps she may be, though I see no proofs of such grim paternity written in her countenance: Pilot is more like me than she.

"Some years after I had broken with the mother, she abandoned her child, and ran away to Italy with a musician or singer. I acknowledged no natural claim on Adele's part to be supported by me, nor do I now acknowledge any, for I am not her father; but hearing that she was quite destitute, I took the poor thing out of the slime and mud of Paris, and transplanted it here, to grow up clean in the wholesome soil of an English country garden.

"Mrs. Fairfax found you to train her; but now you know that she is the illegitimate offspring of a French opera girl, you will perhaps think differently of your post and protegee: you will be coming to me some day with notice that you have found another place—that you beg me to look out for a new governess?

"No: Adele is not answerable for either her mother's faults or yours: I have a regard for her; and now that I know she is, in a sense, parentless—forsaken by her mother and disowned by you, sir— I shall cling closer to her than before. How could I possibly prefer the spoilt pet of a wealthy family, who would hate her governess as a nuisance, to a lonely little orphan, who leans towards her as a friend? Oh, that is the light in which you view it! Well, I must go in now; and you too: it darkens."

After I had withdrawn to my own chamber for the night, that I steadily reviewed the tale Mr. Rochester had told me. As he had said, there was probably nothing at all extraordinary in the substance of the narrative itself: a wealthy Englishman's passion for a French dancer, and her treachery to him, were everyday matters enough, no doubt, in society; but there was something decidedly strange in the paroxysm of emotion which had suddenly seized him when he was in the act of expressing the present contentment of his mood, and his newly revived pleasure in the old hall and its environs.

I meditated wonderingly on this incident; but gradually quitting it, as I found it for the present inexplicable, I turned to the consideration of my master's manner to myself. The confidence he had thought fit to repose in me seemed a tribute to my discretion: I regarded and accepted it as such. His deportment had now for some weeks been more uniform towards me than at the first.

I never seemed in his way; he did not take fits of chilling hauteur: when he met me unexpectedly, the encounter seemed welcome; he had always a word and sometimes a smile for me: when summoned by formal invitation to his presence, I was honored by a cordiality of reception that made me feel I really possessed the power to amuse him, and that these evening conferences were sought as much for his pleasure as for my benefit.

I, indeed, talked comparatively little, but I heard him talk with relish. It was his nature to be communicative; he liked to open to a mind unacquainted with the world glimpses of its scenes and ways. I had a keen delight in receiving the new ideas he offered, in imagining the new pictures he portrayed, and following him in thought through the new regions he disclosed.

The ease of his manner freed me from painful restraint: the friendly frankness, as correct as cordial, with which he treated me, drew me to him. I felt at times as if he were my relation rather than my master: yet he was imperious sometimes still; but I did not mind that; I saw it was his way. So happy, so gratified did I become with this new interest added to life, that I ceased to pine after kindred: my thin crescent destiny seemed to enlarge; the blanks of existence were filled up; my bodily health improved; I gathered strength.

And was Mr. Rochester now ugly in my eyes? No, reader: gratitude, and many associations, all pleasurable and genial, made his face the object I best liked to see; his presence in a room was more cheering than the brightest fire. Yet I had not forgotten his faults; indeed, I could not, for he brought them frequently before me.

He was proud, sardonic, harsh to inferiority of every description: in my secret soul I knew that his great kindness to me was balanced by unjust severity to many others. He was moody, too; unaccountably so; I more than once, when sent for to read to him, found him sitting in his library alone, with his head bent on his folded arms; and, when he looked up, a morose, almost a malignant, scowl blackened his features.

But I believed that his moodiness, his harshness, and his former faults of morality (I say FORMER, for now he seemed corrected of them) had their source in some cruel cross of fate. I believed he was naturally a man of better tendencies, higher principles, and purer tastes than such as circumstances had developed, education instilled, or destiny encouraged. I thought there were excellent materials in him; though for the present they hung together somewhat spoiled and tangled. I cannot deny that I grieved for his grief, whatever that was, and would have given much to assuage it.

Though I had now extinguished my candle and was laid down in bed, I could not sleep for thinking of his look when he paused in the avenue, and told how his destiny had risen up before him, and dared him to be happy at Thornfield.

"Why not?" I asked myself. "What alienates him from the house? Will he leave it again soon? Mrs. Fairfax said he seldom stayed here longer than a fortnight at a time; and he has now been resident eight weeks. If he does go, the change will be doleful. Suppose he should be absent spring, summer, and autumn: how joyless sunshine and fine days will seem!"

I hardly know whether I had slept or not after this musing; at any rate, I started wide awake on hearing a vague murmur, peculiar and lugubrious, which sounded, I thought, just above me. I wished I had kept my candle burning: the night was drearily dark; my spirits were depressed. I rose and sat up in bed, listening. The sound was hushed.

I tried again to sleep; but my heart beat anxiously: my inward tranquility was broken. The clock, far down in the hall, struck two. Just then it seemed my chamber door was touched; as if fingers had swept the panels in groping a way along the dark gallery outside. I said, "Who is there?" Nothing answered. I was chilled with fear.

All at once I remembered that it might be Pilot, who, when the kitchen door chanced to be left open, not infrequently found his way up to the threshold of Mr. Rochester's chamber: I had seen him lying there myself in the mornings. The idea calmed me somewhat: I lay down. I began to feel the return of slumber. But it was not fated that I should sleep that night. A dream had scarcely started, when it fled affrighted, scared by a marrow freezing incident enough.

This was a demoniac laugh—low, suppressed, and deep— uttered, as it seemed, at the very keyhole of my chamber door. The head of my bed was near the door, and I thought at first the goblin laughter stood at my bedside— or rather, crouched by my pillow: but I rose, looked round, and could see nothing; while, as I still gazed, the unnatural sound repeated: and I knew it came from behind the panels. My first impulse was to rise and fasten the bolt;

my next, again to cry out, "Who is there?"

Something gurgled and moaned. Ere long, steps retreated up the gallery towards the third story staircase. I heard a door open and close, and all was still.

"Was that Grace Poole? and is she possessed with a devil?" thought I. Impossible now to remain longer by myself: I must go to Mrs. Fairfax. I opened the door with a trembling hand. There was a candle burning just outside, and on the matting in the gallery. While looking to the right hand and left, I became aware of a strong smell of burning.

Something creaked: it was a door ajar; and that door was Mr. Rochester's, and the smoke rushed in a cloud from thence. I thought no more of Mrs. Fairfax. In an instant, I was within the chamber. Tongues of flame darted round the bed: the curtains were on fire. In the midst of blaze and vapor, Mr. Rochester lay stretched motionless, in deep sleep.

"Wake! wake!" I cried. I shook him, but he only murmured and turned: the smoke had stupefied him. Not a moment could be lost: the very sheets were kindling, I rushed to his basin. Fortunately, it was filled with water. I heaved it, deluged the bed and its occupant, flew back to my own room, brought my own water jug, and by God's aid, succeeded in extinguishing the flames which were devouring it.

The hiss of the quenched element, the breakage of a pitcher which I flung from my hand when I had emptied it, and, above all, the splash of the shower bath I had liberally bestowed, roused Mr. Rochester at last. I heard him fulminating strange anathemas.

"Is there a flood?" he cried. "No, sir," I answered; "but there has been a fire: get up, do; you are quenched now; I will fetch you a candle."

"In the name of all the elves in Christendom, is that Jane Eyre?" he demanded. "What have you done with me, witch, sorceress? Who is in the room besides you? Have you plotted to drown me?"

"I will fetch you a candle, sir; and, in Heaven's name, get up. Somebody has plotted something: you cannot too soon find out who and what it is."

"There! Fetch a candle. Now run!"

I did run; I brought the candle which still remained in the gallery. He took it from my hand, held it up, and surveyed the bed, all blackened and scorched, the sheets drenched, the carpet round swimming in water.

"What is it? and who did it?" he asked. I briefly related to him what had transpired: the strange laugh I had heard in the gallery: the step ascending to the third story; the smoke,—the smell of fire which had conducted me to his room, and how I had deluged him with all the water I could lay my hands on.

He listened very gravely; his face, as I went on, expressed more concern than astonishment; he did not immediately speak when I had concluded.

"Shall I call Mrs. Fairfax?" I asked.

"No. What can she do? Let her sleep. I am going to leave you a few minutes. I shall take the candle. Remain where you are till I return. I must pay a visit to the second story. Don't move, or call anyone."

He went: I watched the light withdraw. He passed up the gallery very softly. I was left in total darkness. I listened for some noise, but heard nothing. A very long time elapsed. I grew weary: it was cold, and then I did not see the use of staying, as I was not to rouse the house. I was on the point of risking Mr. Rochester's displeasure by disobeying his orders, when the light once more gleamed dimly on the gallery wall. "I hope it is he," thought I, "and not something worse."

He re-entered, pale and very gloomy. "I have found it all out," said he, setting his candle down on the washstand; "it is as I thought."

"How, sir?" He made no reply, but stood with his arms folded, looking on the ground. He inquired in rather a peculiar tone—

"I forget whether you said you saw anything when you opened your chamber door."

"No, sir, only the candlestick on the ground."

"But you heard an odd laugh? You have heard that laugh before, I should think, or something like it?"

"Yes, sir: there is a woman who sews here, called Grace Poole,—she laughs in that way."

"Just so. Grace Poole—you have guessed it. She is singular—very. I am glad that you are the only person, besides myself, acquainted with the precise details of tonight's incident. Say nothing about it. Now return to your own room. I shall do very well on the sofa in the library for the rest of the night. It is near four: in two hours the servants will be up."

"Goodnight, then, sir," said I, departing. He seemed surprised—very inconsistently so, as he had just told me to go.

"What!" he exclaimed, "are you quitting me already, and in that way?"

"You said I might go, sir."

"But not without taking leave; not without a word or two of acknowledgment and goodwill: not, in that brief, dry fashion. Why, you have saved my life!—snatched me from a horrible and excruciating death! and you walk past me as if we were mutual strangers! At least shake hands."

He held out his hand; I gave him mine: he took it first in one, them in both his own.

"You have saved my life: I have a pleasure in owing you so immense a debt. I cannot say more. Nothing else that has being would have been tolerable to me in the character of creditor for such an obligation: but you: it is different;—I feel your benefits no burden, Jane."

He paused; gazed at me: words almost visible trembled on his lips,but his voice was checked.

"Goodnight again, sir. There is no debt, benefit, burden, obligation."

"I knew," he continued, "you would do me good in some way, at some time;—I saw it in your eyes when I first beheld you: their expression and smile did not"—(again he stopped)—"did not strike delight to my very inmost heart so for nothing. People talk of natural sympathies; I have heard of good genii: there are grains of truth in the wildest fable. My cherished preserver, goodnight!"

Strange energy was in his voice, strange fire in his look.

"I am glad I happened to be awake," I said: and then I was going.

"What! you WILL go?"

"I am cold, sir."

"Cold? Yes. Go, then, Jane; go!" But he still retained my hand, and I had trouble freeing it.

I both wished and feared to see Mr. Rochester on the day which followed this sleepless night: I wanted to hear his voice again, yet feared to meet his eye. During the early part of the morning, I momentarily expected his coming; he was not in the frequent habit of entering the schoolroom, but he did step in for a few minutes sometimes, and I had the impression that he was sure to visit it that day. But the morning passed just as usual: nothing happened to interrupt the quiet course of Adele's studies.

[[Jane wondered what hold Grace Poole had over Mr. Rochester. She wondered how on a brief encounter with Grace Poole, the woman could seem rational yet a nocturnal fiend.]]

[[Jane heard that Mr. Rochester was traveling and consorting with a young woman, Miss Ingram.]]

When once more alone, I reviewed the information I had got; looked into my heart, examined its thoughts and feelings, and endeavored to bring back the safe fold of common sense. I pronounced judgment to this effect-

That a greater fool than Jane Eyre had never breathed the breath of life; that a more fantastic idiot had never surfeited herself on sweet lies, and swallowed poison as if it were nectar.

"YOU," I said, "a favorite with Mr. Rochester? YOU gifted with the power of pleasing him? YOU of importance to him in any way? And you have derived pleasure from occasional tokens of preference— equivocal tokens shown by a gentleman of family and a man of the world to a dependent and a novice. How dared you? Poor stupid dupe!—Could not even self interest make you wiser?

"You repeated to yourself this morning the brief scene of last night? It does good to no woman to be flattered by her superior, who cannot possibly intend to marry her; and it is madness in all women to let a secret love kindle within them, which, if unreturned and unknown, must devour the life that feeds it; and, if discovered and responded to, must lead into miry wilds whence there is no extrication."

[[Mr Rochester was away for two weeks. Jane found herself longing for his return. A letter announced that he would be returning and that preparations needed to be made for several house guests.]]

A joyous stir was now audible in the hall: gentlemen's deep tones and ladies' silvery accents blent harmoniously together, and distinguishable above all, though not loud, was the sonorous voice of the master of Thornfield Hall, welcoming guests.

[[Jane observed Mr. Rochester's high society company and stayed in the background.]]

And did I now think Miss Ingram such a choice as Mr. Rochester would be likely to make? I could not tell—I did not know his taste in female beauty. If he liked the majestic, she was the very type of majesty: then she was accomplished, sprightly. Most gentlemen would admire her, I thought; and that he DID admire her, I already seemed to have obtained proof: to remove the last shade of doubt, it remained but to see them together.

[[Jane's feelings for Mr. Rochester resurfaced.]]

Did I say, a few days since, that I had nothing to do with him but to receive my salary at his hands? Did I forbid myself to think of him in any other light than as a paymaster? Every good, true, vigorous feeling I have gathers impulsively round him. I know I must conceal my sentiments: I must smother hope; I must remember that he cannot care much for me. For when I say that I am of his kind, I do not mean that I have his force to influence, and his spell to attract; I mean only that I have certain tastes and feelings in common with him. I must, then, repeat continually that we are for ever sundered:- and yet, while I breathe and think, I must love him."

[[Jane observed Miss Ingram and Mr. Rochester together. Jane watched as Miss Ingram played the piano while Mr. Rochester sang.]]

"Now is my time to slip away," thought I: but the tones that then severed the air arrested me. Mrs. Fairfax had said Mr. Rochester possessed a fine voice: he did—a mellow, powerful bass, into which he threw his own feeling, his own force; finding a way through the ear to the heart, and there waking sensation strangely. I waited till the last deep and full vibration had expired. A gentleman came out. I stood face to face with Mr. Rochester.

"How do you do?" he asked.

"I am very well, sir."

"Why did you not come and speak to me in the room?" I thought I might have retorted the question on him who put it: but I would not take that freedom. I answered—

"I did not wish to disturb you, as you seemed engaged, sir."

"What have you been doing during my absence?"

"Nothing particular; teaching Adele as usual."

"And getting a good deal paler than you were—as I saw at first sight. What is the matter?"

"Nothing at all, sir."

"Did you take any cold that night you half drowned me?"

"Not the least."

"Return to the drawing room: you are deserting too early."

"I am tired, sir." He looked at me for a minute. "And a little depressed," he said. "What about? Tell me."

"Nothing—nothing, sir. I am not depressed."

"But I affirm that you are: so much depressed that a few more words would bring tears to your eyes—indeed, they are there now, shining and swimming; and a bead has slipped from the lash and fallen on to the stone. If I had time, and was not in mortal dread of some prating prig of a servant passing, I would know what all this means. Well, tonight I excuse you; but understand that so long as my visitors stay, I expect you to appear in the drawing room every evening; it is my wish; don't neglect it. Now go, and send Sophie for Adele. Goodnight, my—" He stopped, bit his lip, and abruptly left me.

Merry days were these at Thornfield Hall; and busy days too: how different from the first three months of stillness, monotony, and solitude I had passed beneath its roof! All sad feelings seemed now driven from the house, all gloomy associations forgotten: there was life everywhere, movement all day long. You could not now traverse the gallery, once so hushed, nor enter the front chambers, once so tenantless, without encountering a smart lady's maid or a dandy valet.

[[Jane's assessment of Miss Ingram —]]

I see Mr. Rochester turn to Miss Ingram, and Miss Ingram to him; I see her incline her head towards him, till her curls almost touch his shoulder and wave against his cheek; I hear their mutual whisperings; I recall their interchanged glances.

I have told you, reader, that I had learnt to love Mr. Rochester: I could not unlove him now, merely because I found that he had ceased to notice me—because I might pass hours in his presence, and he would never once turn his eyes in my direction—because I saw all his attentions appropriated by a great lady, who scorned to touch me with the hem of her robes as she passed; who, if ever her dark and imperious eye fell on me by chance, would withdraw it instantly as from an object too mean to merit observation.

I could not unlove him, because I felt sure he would soon marry this very lady—because I read daily in her a proud security in his intentions respecting her—because I witnessed hourly in him a style of courtship which, if careless and choosing rather to be sought than to seek, was yet, in its very carelessness, captivating, and in its very pride, irresistible.

There was nothing to cool or banish love in these circumstances, though much to create despair. Much too, you will think, reader, to engender jealousy: if a woman, in my position, could presume to be jealous of a woman in Miss Ingram's. But I was not jealous: or very rarely;—the nature of the pain I suffered could not be explained by that word. Miss Ingram was a mark beneath jealousy: she was too inferior to excite the feeling.

Pardon the seeming paradox; I mean what I say. She was very showy, but she was not genuine: she had a fine person, many brilliant attainments; but her mind was poor, her heart barren by nature: nothing bloomed spontaneously on that soil; no unforced natural fruit delighted by its freshness. She was not good; she was not original: she used to repeat sounding phrases from books: she never offered, nor had, an opinion of her own.

She advocated a high tone of sentiment; but she did not know the sensations of sympathy and pity; tenderness and truth were not in her. Too often she betrayed this, by the undue vent she gave to a spiteful antipathy she had conceived against little Adele: pushing her away with some contemptuous epithet if she happened to approach her; sometimes ordering her from the room, and always treating her with coldness and acrimony.

Other eyes besides mine watched these manifestations of character—watched them closely, keenly, shrewdly. Yes; the future bridegroom, Mr. Rochester himself, exercised over his intended a ceaseless surveillance; and it was from this sagacity—this guardedness of his—this perfect, clear consciousness of his fair one's defects— this obvious absence of passion in his sentiments towards her, that my ever torturing pain arose.

I saw he was going to marry her, for family, perhaps political reasons, because her rank and connections suited him; I felt he had not given her his love, and that her qualifications were ill adapted to win from him that treasure. This was the point—this was where the nerve was touched and teased—this was where the fever was sustained and fed: SHE COULD NOT CHARM HIM.

If she had managed the victory at once, and he had yielded and sincerely laid his heart at her feet, I should have covered my face, turned to the wall, and (figuratively) have died to them. If Miss Ingram had been a good and noble woman, endowed with force, fervor, kindness, sense, I should have had one vital struggle with two tigers—jealousy and despair: then, my heart torn out and devoured, I should have admired her—acknowledged her excellence, and been quiet for the rest of my days: and the more absolute her superiority, the deeper would have been my admiration—the more truly tranquil my quiescence.

But as matters really stood, to watch Miss Ingram's efforts at fascinating Mr. Rochester, to witness their repeated failure—herself unconscious that they did fail; vainly fancying that each shaft launched hit the mark, and infatuatedly pluming herself on success, when her pride and self complacency repelled further and further what she wished to allure—to witness THIS, was to be at once under ceaseless excitation and ruthless restraint.

"Why can she not influence him more, when she is privileged to draw so near to him?" I asked myself. "It seems to me that she might, by merely sitting quietly at his side, saying little and looking less, get nigher his heart. I have seen in his face a far different expression from that which hardens it now while she is so vivaciously accosting him. How will she manage to please him when they are married? I do not think she will manage it; and yet it might be managed; and his wife might, I verily believe, be the very happiest woman the sun shines on."

I have not yet said anything condemnatory of Mr. Rochester's project of marrying for interest and connections. It surprised me when I first discovered that such was his intention: I had thought him a man unlikely to be influenced by motives so commonplace in his choice of a wife; but the longer I considered the position, education, etc., of the parties, the less I felt justified in judging and blaming either him or Miss Ingram for acting in conformity to ideas and principles instilled into them, doubtless, from their childhood.

All their class held these principles: I supposed, then, they had reasons for holding them such as I could not fathom. It seemed to me that, were I a gentleman like him, I would take only such a wife as I could love; but the very obviousness of the advantages to the husband's own happiness offered by this plan convinced me that there must be arguments against its general adoption of which I was quite ignorant: otherwise I felt sure all the world would act as I wished to act.

But in other points, as well as this, I was growing very lenient to my master: I was forgetting all his faults, for which I had once kept a sharp lookout. It had formerly been my endeavor to study all sides of his character: to take the bad with the good; and from the just weighing of both, to form an equitable judgment. Now I saw no bad. The sarcasm that had repelled, the harshness that had startled me once, were only like keen condiments in a choice dish: their presence was pungent, but their absence would be felt as comparatively insipid.

And his sorrowful expression that opened and closed again before one could fathom the strange depth partially disclosed; that something which used to make me fear and shrink, as if I had been wandering amongst volcanic looking hills, and had suddenly felt the ground quiver and seen it gape: that something, I, at intervals, beheld still; and with throbbing heart. Instead of wishing to shun, I longed only to dare—to divine it. O, to look into the abyss, explore its secrets and analyze its nature.

Meantime, while I thought only of my master and his future bride— saw only them, heard only their discourse, and considered only their movements of importance—the rest of the party were occupied with their own separate interests and pleasures.

[[While Mr. Rochester went to town, another guest arrived. That evening a gypsy fortuneteller pestered at the door to read fortunes for the young ladies

30

present. The gypsy requested that Jane consult with her.]]

I was glad of the unexpected opportunity to gratify my much excited curiosity.

"Well, and you want your fortune told?" she said, in a voice as decided as her glance, as harsh as her features.

"I don't care about it, mother; you may please yourself: but I ought to warn you, I have no faith."

"It's like your impudence to say so: I expected it of you; I heard it in your step as you crossed the threshold."

"Did you? You've a quick ear."

"I have; and a quick eye and a quick brain."

"You need them all in your trade."

"I do; especially when I've customers like you to deal with. Why don't you tremble?"

"I'm not cold."

"Why don't you turn pale?"

"I am not sick."

"Why don't you consult my art?"

"I'm not silly." The old crone 'nichered' a laugh. She then drew out a short black pipe, and lighting it began to smoke. Having indulged a while in this sedative, she raised her bent body, took the pipe from her lips, and while gazing steadily at the fire, said very deliberately—

"You are cold; you are sick; and you are silly."

"Prove it," I rejoined.

"I will, in few words. You are cold, because you are alone: no contact strikes the fire from you that is in you. You are sick; because the best of feelings, the highest and the sweetest given to man, keeps far away from you. You are silly, because, suffer as you may, you will not beckon it to approach, nor will you stir one step to meet it where it waits you."

She again put her short black pipe to her lips, and renewed her smoking with vigor.

"You might say all that to almost any one who you knew lived as a solitary dependent in a great house."

"I might say it to almost any one: but would it be true of almost any one?"

"In my circumstances."

"Yes; just so, in YOUR circumstances: but find me another precisely placed as you are."

"It would be easy to find you thousands."

"You could scarcely find me one. If you knew it, you are peculiarly situated: very near happiness; yes, within reach of it. The materials are all prepared; there only wants a movement to combine them."

"I don't understand enigmas. I never could guess a riddle in my life."

"If you wish me to speak more plainly, show me your palm."

"And I must cross it with silver, I suppose?"

"To be sure."

I gave her a shilling. She told me to hold out my hand. I did. She ached her face to the palm, and pored over it without touching it.

"It is too fine," said she. "I can make nothing of such a hand as that; almost without lines: besides, what is in a palm? Destiny is not written there."

"I believe you," said I.

"No," she continued, "it is in the face, about the eyes, in the lines of the mouth. Kneel, and lift up your head."

I knelt within half a yard of her. She stirred the fire, so that a ripple of light broke from the disturbed coal: the glare, however, as she sat, only threw her face into deeper shadow: mine, it illumined.

"I wonder with what feelings you came to me tonight," she said, when she had examined me a while. "I wonder what thoughts are busy in your heart during all the hours you sit in yonder room with the fine people flitting before you like shapes in a magic lantern: just as little sympathetic communion passing between you and them as if they were really mere shadows of human forms, and not the actual substance."

"I feel tired often, sleepy sometimes, but seldom sad."

"Then you have some secret hope to buoy you up and please you with whispers of the future?"

"Not I. The utmost I hope is, to save money enough out of my earnings to set up a school some day in a little house rented by myself."

"A mean nutriment for the spirit to exist on: and you sitting in that window seat (you see I know your habits)—"

"You have learned them from the servants."

"Ah! you think yourself sharp. Well, perhaps I have: to speak truth, I have an acquaintance with one of them, Mrs. Poole—"

I started to my feet when I heard the name. "You have—have you?" thought I; "there is diablerie in the business after all, then!"

"Don't be alarmed," continued the strange being; "she's a safe hand is Mrs. Poole: close and quiet; any one may repose confidence in her. But, as I was saying: sitting in that window seat, do you think of nothing but your future school? Have you no present interest in any of the company who occupy the sofas and chairs before you? Is there not one face you study? one figure whose movements you follow with at least curiosity?"

"I like to observe all the faces and all the figures."

"But do you never single one from the rest—or it may be, two?"

"I do frequently; when the gestures or looks of a pair seem telling a tale: it amuses me to watch them."

"What tale do you like best to hear?"

"Oh, I have not much choice! They generally run on the same theme—courtship; and promise to end in the same catastrophe—marriage."

"And do you like that monotonous theme?"

"Positively, I don't care about it: it is nothing to me."

"Nothing to you? When a lady, young and full of life and health, charming with beauty and endowed with the gifts of rank and fortune, sits and smiles in the eyes of a gentleman you—"

"I what?"

"You know—and perhaps think well of."

"I don't know the gentlemen here. I have scarcely interchanged a syllable with one of them; and as to thinking well of them, I consider some respectable, and stately, and middle aged, and others young, dashing, handsome, and lively: but certainly they are all at liberty to be the recipients of whose smiles they please, without my feeling disposed to consider the transaction of any moment to me."

"You don't know the gentlemen here? You have not exchanged a syllable with one of them? Will you say that of the master of the house!"

"He is not at home."

"A profound remark! A most ingenious quibble! He went to Millcote this morning, and will be back here tonight or tomorrow: does that circumstance exclude him from the list of your acquaintance— blot him, as it were, out of existence?"

"No; but I can scarcely see what Mr. Rochester has to do with the theme you had introduced."

"I was talking of ladies smiling in the eyes of gentlemen; and of late so many smiles have been shed into Mr. Rochester's eyes that they overflow like two cups filled above the brim: have you never remarked that?"

"Mr. Rochester has a right to enjoy the society of his guests."

"No question about his right: but have you never observed that, of all the tales told here about matrimony, Mr. Rochester has been favored with the most lively and the most continuous?"

"The eagerness of a listener quickens the tongue of a narrator." I said this rather to myself than to the gypsy, whose strange talk, voice, manner, had by this time wrapped me in a kind of dream. One unexpected sentence came from her lips after another, till I got involved in a web of mystification; and wondered what unseen spirit had been sitting for weeks by my heart watching its workings and taking record of every pulse.

"Eagerness of a listener!" repeated she: "yes; Mr. Rochester has sat by the hour, his ear inclined to the fascinating lips that took such delight in their task of communicating; and Mr. Rochester was so willing to receive and looked so grateful for the pastime given him; you have noticed this?"

"Grateful! I cannot remember detecting gratitude in his face."

"Detecting! You have analyzed, then. And what did you detect, if not gratitude?"

I said nothing. "You have seen love: have you not?—and, looking forward, you have seen him married, and beheld his bride happy?"

"Not exactly. Your witch's skill is rather at fault sometimes."

"What the devil have you seen, then?"

"Never mind: I came here to inquire, not to confess. Is it known that Mr. Rochester is to be married?"

"Yes; and to the beautiful Miss Ingram."

"Shortly?"

"Appearances would warrant that conclusion: and, no doubt (though, with an audacity that wants chastising out of you, you seem to question it), they will be a superlatively happy pair. He must love such a handsome, noble, witty, accomplished lady; and probably she loves him, or, if not his person, at least his purse. I know she considers the Rochester estate eligible to the last degree; though (God pardon me!) I told her something on that point about an hour ago which made her look wondrous grave: the corners of her mouth fell half an inch. I would advise her blackaviced suitor to look out: if another comes, with a longer or clearer rent roll,—he's dished—"

"But, mother, I did not come to hear Mr. Rochester's fortune: I came to hear my own; and you have told me nothing of it."

"Your fortune is yet doubtful: when I examined your face, one trait contradicted another. Chance has meted you a measure of happiness: that I know. I knew it before I came here this evening. She has laid it carefully on one side for you. I saw her do it. It depends on yourself to stretch out your hand, and take it up: but whether you will do so, is the problem I study. Kneel again on the rug."

"Don't keep me long; the fire scorches me." I knelt. She did not stoop towards me, but only gazed, leaning back in her chair. She began muttering,—

"The flame flickers in the eye; the eye shines like dew; it looks soft and full of feeling; it smiles at my jargon: it is susceptible; impression follows impression where it ceases to smile, it is sad. That signifies melancholy resulting from loneliness. It turns from me; it will not suffer further scrutiny; it seems to deny, by a mocking glance, the truth of the discoveries I have already made,—to disown the charge both of sensibility and chagrin: its pride and reserve only confirm me in my opinion.

"As to the mouth, it delights at times in laughter; it is disposed to impart all that the brain conceives; though I daresay it would be silent on much the heart experiences. Mobile and flexible, it was never intended to be compressed in the eternal silence of solitude: it is a mouth which should speak much and smile often.

"That brow professes to say,—"I can live alone, if self respect, and circumstances require me so to do. I have an inward treasure born with me, which can keep me alive if all extraneous delights should be withheld, or offered only at a price I cannot afford to give." The forehead declares, "Reason sits firm and holds the reins, and she will not let the feelings burst away and hurry her to wild chasms. The passions may rage furiously, like true heathens, as they are; and the desires may imagine all sorts of vain things: but judgment shall still have the last word in every argument, and the casting vote in every decision. Strong wind, earthquake shock, and fire may pass by: but I shall follow the guiding of that still small voice which interprets the dictates of conscience.

"That will do. I think I rave in a kind of exquisite delirium. I should wish now to protract this moment ad infinitum; but I dare not. So far I have governed myself thoroughly. I have acted as I inwardly swore I would act; but further might try me beyond my strength. Rise, Miss Eyre: leave me; 'the play is played out.'"

Where was I? Did I wake or sleep? Had I been dreaming? Did I dream still? The old woman's voice had changed: her accent, her gesture, and all were familiar to me as my own face in a glass—as the speech of my own tongue. I got up, but did not go. I looked but she drew her bonnet closer about her face, and again beckoned me to depart. The flame illuminated her hand. A ring flashed on the little finger, and stooping forward, I looked at it, and saw a gem I had seen a hundred times before. Again I looked at the face; which was no longer turned from me—on the contrary, the bonnet was doffed.

"Well, Jane, do you know me?" asked the familiar voice.

"Only take off the red cloak, sir, and then—"

"But the string is in a knot—help me."

"Break it, sir."

And Mr. Rochester stepped out of his disguise.

"Now, sir, what a strange idea!"

"But well carried out, eh? Don't you think so?"

"With the ladies you must have managed well."

"But not with you?"

"You did not act the character of a gypsy with me."

"What character did I act? My own?"

"No; some unaccountable one. In short, I believe you have been trying to draw me out—or in; you have been talking nonsense to make me talk nonsense. It is scarcely fair, sir."

"Do you forgive me, Jane?"

"I cannot tell till I have thought it all over. If, on reflection, I find I have fallen into no great absurdity, I shall try to forgive you; but it was not right."

"Oh, you have been very correct—very careful, very sensible."

I reflected, and thought, on the whole, I had. It was a comfort; but, indeed, I had been on my guard almost from the beginning of the interview. Something of masquerade I suspected. I knew gypsies and fortune tellers did not express themselves as this seeming old woman had expressed herself; besides I had noted her feigned voice, her anxiety to conceal her features. But my mind had been running on Grace Poole—that living enigma, that mystery of mysteries, as I considered her. I had never thought of Mr. Rochester.

"Well," said he, "what are you musing about? What does that grave smile signify?"

"Wonder and self congratulation, sir. I have your permission to retire now, I suppose?"

"No; stay a moment; and tell me what the people in the drawing room yonder are doing."

"Discussing the gypsy, I daresay."

"Sit down!—Let me hear what they said about me."

"I had better not stay long, sir; it must be near eleven o"clock. Oh, are you aware, Mr. Rochester, that a stranger has arrived here since you left this morning?"

"A stranger!—no; who can it be? I expected no one."

"He said he had known you long, and that he could take the liberty of installing himself here till you returned."

"The devil he did! Did he give his name?"

"His name is Mason, sir; and he comes from the West Indies; from Spanish

Town, in Jamaica, I think."

Mr. Rochester was standing near me; he had taken my hand, as if to lead me to a chair. As I spoke he gave my wrist a convulsive grip; the smile on his lips froze.

"Mason!—the West Indies!" he said.

"Do you feel ill, sir?" I inquired.

"Jane, I've got a blow; I've got a blow, Jane!" He staggered.

"Oh, lean on me, sir."

"Jane, you offered me your shoulder once before; let me have it now."

"Yes, sir, yes; and my arm." He sat down, and made me sit beside him. Holding my hand in both his own with the most troubled and dreary look.

"My little friend!" said he, "I wish I were in a quiet island with only you; and trouble, and danger, and hideous recollections removed from me."

"Can I help you, sir?—I"d give my life to serve you."

"Jane, if aid is wanted, I'll seek it at your hands; I promise you that."

"Thank you, sir. Tell me what to do,—I'll try, at least, to do it."

"Fetch me now, Jane, a glass of wine from the dining room: they will be at supper there; and tell me if Mason is with them, and what he is doing."

I went and found all the party in the dining room at supper. They stood about in groups, their plates and glasses in their hands. Every one seemed in high glee; laughter and conversation were general and animated. Mr. Mason stood near the fire, talking to Colonel and Mrs. Dent, and appeared as merry as any of them. I filled a wine glass (I saw Miss Ingram watch me frowningly as I did so: she thought I was taking a liberty, I daresay), and I returned to the library.

Mr. Rochester's extreme pallor had disappeared, and he looked once more firm and stern. He took the glass from my hand.

He swallowed the contents and returned it to me. "What are they doing, Jane?"

"Laughing and talking, sir."

"They don't look grave and mysterious, as if they had heard something strange?"

"Not at all: they are full of jests and gaiety."

"And Mason?"

"He was laughing too."

"If all these people came in a body and spat at me, what would you do, Jane?"

"Turn them out of the room, sir, if I could."

He half smiled. "But if I were to go to them, and they only looked at me coldly, and whispered sneeringly amongst each other, and then dropped off and left me one by one, what then? Would you go with them?"

"I rather think not, sir: I should have more pleasure in staying with you."

"To comfort me?"

"Yes, sir, to comfort you, as well as I could."

"And if they laid you under a ban for adhering to me?"

"I, probably, should know nothing about their ban; and if I did, I should care nothing about it."

"Then, you could dare censure for my sake?"

"I could dare it for the sake of any friend who deserved my adherence; as you, I am sure, do."

"Go back now into the room; step quietly up to Mason, and whisper in his ear that Mr. Rochester is come and wishes to see him: show him in here and then leave me."

"Yes, sir." I did his behest. The company all stared at me as I passed straight among them. I sought Mr. Mason, delivered the message, and preceded him from the room: I ushered him into the library, and then I went upstairs.

At a late hour, after I had been in bed some time, I heard the visitors repair to their chambers: I distinguished Mr. Rochester's voice, and heard him say, "This way, Mason; this is your room."

He spoke cheerfully: the gay tones set my heart at ease. I was soon asleep.

I had forgotten to draw my curtain, which I usually did, and also to let down my window blind. The consequence was, that when the moon, which was full and bright, came in her course to that space in the sky opposite my casement. Awaking in the dead of night, I opened my eyes on her disk—silver white and crystal clear. It was beautiful, but too solemn. I stretched my arm to draw the curtain.

Good God! What a cry! The night—its silence—its rest, was rent in twain by a savage, a sharp, a shrilly sound that ran from end to end of Thornfield Hall.

My pulse stopped: my heart stood still; my stretched arm was paralyzed The cry died, and was not renewed. Indeed, whatever being uttered that fearful shriek could not soon repeat it: not the widest winged condor on the Andes could, twice in succession, send out such a yell.

It came out of the third story; for it passed overhead. And overhead—yes, in the room just above my chamber ceiling—I now heard a struggle: a deadly one it seemed from the noise; and a half smothered voice shouted—

"Help! help! help!" three times rapidly. "Will no one come?" it cried; and then, while the staggering and stamping went on wildly, I distinguished through plank and plaster:-

"Rochester! Rochester! for God's sake, come!" A chamber door opened: some one ran, or rushed, along the gallery. Another step stamped on the flooring above and something fell; and there was silence.

I had put on some clothes, though horror shook all my limbs. The sleepers were all aroused: terrified murmurs sounded in every room; doors opened; one looked out and another looked out; the gallery filled. "Oh! what is it?"—"Who is hurt?"—"What has happened?"—"Fetch a light!"—"Is it fire?"— "Are there robbers?"—"Where shall we run?" was demanded confusedly on all hands. But for the moonlight they would have been in complete darkness. They ran to and fro; they crowded together: some sobbed, some stumbled, confusion reigned.

"Where the devil is Rochester?" cried Colonel Dent. "I cannot find him in his bed."

"Here! here!" was shouted in return. "Be composed, all of you: I'm coming."

And the door at the end of the gallery opened, and Mr. Rochester advanced with a candle: he had just descended from the upper story One of the ladies ran to him directly; she seized his arm: it was Miss Ingram.

"What awful event has taken place?" said she. "Speak! let us know the worst at once!"

"But don't pull me down or strangle me," he replied: for the Misses Eshton were clinging about him now; and the two dowagers, in vast white robes, were bearing down on him like ships in full sail.

"All's right!—all's right!" he cried. "It's a mere rehearsal of Much Ado about Nothing. Ladies, keep off, or I shall wax dangerous."

And dangerous he looked: his black eyes darted sparks. Calming himself by an effort, he added—

"A servant has had the nightmare; that is all. She's an excitable, nervous person. Now, then, I must see you all back into your rooms; for, till the house is settled, she cannot be looked after."

And so, by dint of alternate coaxing and commanding, he contrived to get them all once more back to their rooms. I did not wait to be ordered back to mine, but retreated unnoticed.

Not, however, to go to bed: on the contrary, I began and dressed myself carefully. The sounds I had heard after the scream, and the words that had been uttered, had probably been heard only by me; for they had proceeded from the room above mine: but they assured me that it was not a servant's dream which had thus struck horror through the house; and that the explanation Mr. Rochester had given was merely an invention framed to pacify his guests. I dressed, then, to be ready for emergencies. When dressed, I sat a long time by the window looking out over the silent grounds and silvered fields and waiting for I knew not what. It seemed to me that some event must follow the strange cry, struggle, and call.

No: stillness returned: each murmur and movement ceased gradually, and in about an hour Thornfield Hall was again as hushed as a desert. It seemed that sleep and night had resumed their empire. The moon declined: she was about to set. Not liking to sit in the cold and darkness, I thought I would lie down on my bed. A cautious hand tapped low at the door.

"Am I wanted?" I asked.

"Are you up?" asked my master.

"Yes, sir."

"And dressed?"

"Yes."

"Come out, then, quietly." Mr. Rochester stood in the gallery holding a light.

He glided up the gallery and up the stairs, and stopped in the dark, low corridor of the fateful third story: I had followed and stood at his side.

[[Mr. Rochester took Jane to a concealed room where she helped with Mr.

Mason who was wounded. Mr. Rochester instructed Jane —]]

"Remember!—No conversation," he left the room.

I experienced a strange feeling as the key grated in the lock, and the sound of his retreating step ceased to be heard. Here then I was in the third story, fastened into one of its mystic cells; night around me; a pale and bloody spectacle under my eyes and hands; a murderess hardly separated from me by a single door: yes—that was appalling—the rest I could bear; but I shuddered at the thought of Grace Poole bursting out upon me.

Amidst all this, I had to listen and watch for the movements of the wild beast or the fiend in yonder side den. But since Mr. Rochester's visit it seemed spellbound: all the night I heard but three sounds at three long intervals,—a step creak, a momentary renewal of the snarling, canine noise, and a deep human groan.

Then my own thoughts worried me. What crime was this that lived incarnate in this sequestered mansion, and could neither be expelled nor subdued by the owner?—what mystery, that broke out now in fire and now in blood, at the deadest hours of night? What creature was it, that, masked in an ordinary woman's face and shape, uttered the voice, now of a mocking demon, and anon of a carrion seeking bird of prey?

And this man I bent over—this commonplace, quiet stranger—how had he become involved in the web of horror? and why had the Fury flown at him? What made him seek this quarter of the house at an untimely season, when he should have been asleep in bed? I had heard Mr. Rochester assign him an apartment below—what brought him here! And why, now, was he so tame under the violence or treachery done him? Why did he so quietly submit to the concealment Mr. Rochester enforced?

Why DID Mr. Rochester enforce this concealment? His guest had been outraged, his own life on a former occasion had been hideously plotted against; and both attempts he smothered in secrecy and sank in oblivion! Lastly, I saw Mr. Mason was submissive to Mr. Rochester; that the impetuous will of the latter held complete sway over the inertness of the former: the few words which had passed between them assured me of this.

It was evident that in their former dialogue, the passive disposition of the one had been habitually influenced by the active energy of the other: whence then had arisen Mr. Rochester's dismay when he heard of Mr. Mason's arrival? Why had the mere name of this unresisting individual—whom his word now sufficed to control like a child—fallen on him, a few hours since, as a thunderbolt might fall on an oak?

Oh! I could not forget his look and his paleness when he whispered: "Jane, I have got a blow—I have got a blow, Jane." I could not forget how the arm had trembled which he rested on my shoulder: and it was no light matter which could thus bow the resolute spirit and thrill the vigorous frame of Fairfax Rochester.

"When will he come? When will he come?" I cried inwardly, as the night lingered and lingered—as my bleeding patient drooped, moaned, sickened: and neither day nor aid arrived. I had, again and again, held the water to Mason's white lips; again and again offered him the stimulating salts: my efforts seemed ineffectual: either bodily or mental suffering, or loss of blood, or all three combined, were fast prostrating his strength. He moaned so, and looked so weak, wild, and lost, I feared he was dying; and I might not even speak to him.

The candle, wasted at last, went out; as it expired, I perceived streaks of grey light edging the window curtains: dawn was then approaching. Presently I heard Pilot bark far below, out of his distant kennel in the courtyard: hope revived. Nor was it unwarranted: in five minutes more the grating key, the yielding lock, warned me my watch was relieved. It could not have lasted more than two hours: many a week has seemed shorter.

Mr. Rochester entered, and with him the surgeon he had been to fetch.

"She bit me," Mason murmured. "She worried me like a tigress, when Rochester got the knife from her. It was frightful!" he added, shuddering. "And I did not expect it: she looked so quiet at first."

"I warned you," replied Rochester, "I said—be on your guard when you go near her. Besides, you might have waited till tomorrow, and had me with you: it was mere folly to attempt to visit tonight, and alone."

"I thought I could have done some good."

"You thought! you thought!, however, you have suffered, and are likely to suffer enough for not taking my advice; so I'll say no more."

I saw Mr. Rochester shudder: a singularly marked expression of disgust, horror, hatred, warped his countenance.

"Yet would to God there was an end of all this!" added Mr. Rochester.

[[The wounded mysterious Mr. Mason was shuttled off in a coach before the sun rose the next morning. Stepping toward the orchard Mr. Rochester said –]]

"Come where there is some freshness, for a few moments."

He strayed down a walk edged with boxwood, with apple trees, pear trees, and cherry trees on one side, and a border on the other full of all sorts of old-fashioned flowers, stocks, sweet williams, primroses, pansies, mingled with southernwood, sweet briar, and various fragrant herbs. The sun was just entering the dappled east, and his light illumined the wreathed and dewy orchard trees and shone down the quiet walks under them.

"Jane, will you have a flower?" He gathered a half blown rose, the first on the bush, and offered it to me.

"Thank you, sir."

"Do you like this sunrise, Jane? That sky with its high and light clouds which are sure to melt away as the day waxes warm—this placid and balmy atmosphere?"

"I do, very much."

"You have passed a strange night, Jane."

"Yes, sir."

"And it has made you look pale—were you afraid when I left you alone with Mason?"

"I was afraid of some one coming out of the inner room."

"But I had fastened the door—I had the key in my pocket: I should have been a careless shepherd if I had left a lamb— my pet lamb—so near a wolf's den, unguarded: you were safe."

"Will Grace Poole live here still, sir?"

"Oh yes! don't trouble your self about her—put the thing out of your thoughts."

"Yet it seems to me your life is hardly secure while she stays."

"Never fear—I will take care of myself."

"Is the danger you apprehended last night gone by now, sir?"

"I cannot vouch for that till Mason is out of England: nor even then. To live, for me, Jane, is to stand on a crater crust which may crack and spew fire any day."

"But Mr. Mason seems a man easily led. Your influence, sir, is evidently potent with him: he will never set you at defiance or willfully injure you."

"Oh, no! Mason will not defy me; nor, knowing it, will he hurt me— but, unintentionally, he might in a moment, by one careless word, deprive me, if not of life, yet for ever of happiness."

The arbor was an arch in the wall, lined with ivy; it contained a rustic seat. Mr. Rochester sat.

"Sit," he said; "the bench is long enough for two. You don't hesitate to take a place at my side, do you? Is that wrong, Jane?"

I answered him by assuming it: to refuse would, I felt, have been unwise.

"Now, my little friend, while the sun drinks the dew— while all the flowers in this old garden awake and expand, and the birds fetch their young ones' breakfast, and the early bees do their first spell of work— I'll put a case to you, which you must endeavor to suppose your own: but first, look at me, and tell me you are at ease, and not fearing that I err in detaining you, or that you err in staying."

"No, sir; I am content."

"Well then, Jane, suppose you were no longer a girl well reared and disciplined, but a wild boy indulged from childhood upwards; imagine yourself in a remote foreign land; conceive that you there commit a capital error, no matter of what nature or from what motives, but one whose consequences must follow you through life and taint all your existence. Mind, I don't say a CRIME; I am not speaking of any guilty act which might make the perpetrator amenable to the law: my word is ERROR.

"The results of what you have done become in time to you utterly insupportable; you take measures to obtain relief: unusual measures, but neither unlawful nor culpable. Still you are miserable; for hope has quitted you on the very confines of life: your sun at noon darkens in an eclipse, which you feel will not leave it till the time of setting.

"Bitter and base associations have become the sole food of your memory: you wander here and there, seeking rest in exile: happiness in pleasure—I mean in heartless, sensual pleasure—such as dulls intellect and blights feeling. Heart weary and soul withered, you come home after years of voluntary banishment: you make a new acquaintance—how or where no matter: you find in this stranger much of the good and bright qualities which you have sought for twenty years, and never before encountered; and they are all fresh, healthy, without soil and without taint.

"Such society revives, regenerates: you feel better days come back—higher wishes, purer feelings; you desire to recommence your life, and to spend what remains to you of days in a way more worthy of an immortal being. To attain this end, are you justified in overleaping an obstacle of custom—a mere conventional impediment which neither your conscience sanctifies nor your judgment approves?"

He paused for an answer: and what was I to say? Oh, for some good spirit to suggest a judicious and satisfactory response! The west wind whispered in the ivy round me; but no gentle Ariel borrowed its breath as a medium of speech: the birds sang in the treetops; but their song, however sweet, was inarticulate.

Again Mr. Rochester propounded his query: "Is the wandering and sinful, but now rest seeking and repentant, man justified in daring the world's opinion, in order to attach to him for ever this gentle, gracious, genial stranger, thereby securing his own peace of mind and regeneration of life?"

"Sir," I answered, "a wanderer's repose or a sinner's reformation should never depend on a fellow creature. Men and women die; philosophers falter in wisdom, and Christians in goodness: if any one you know has suffered and erred, let him look higher than his equals for strength to amend and solace to heal."

"But the instrument—the instrument! God, who does the work, ordains the instrument. I have myself—I tell it you without parable—been a worldly, dissipated, restless man; and I believe I have found the instrument for my cure in—" He paused: the birds went on caroling, the leaves lightly rustling. I almost wondered they did not check their songs and whispers to catch the suspended revelation. At last I looked up at Mr. Rochester: he was looking eagerly at me.

"Little friend," said he, in quite a changed tone—while his face changed too, losing all its softness and gravity, and becoming harsh and sarcastic—"you have noticed my tender penchant for Miss Ingram: don't you think if I married her she would regenerate me with a vengeance?"

He got up instantly, went quite to the other end of the walk, and when he came back he was humming a tune.

"Jane, Jane," said he, stopping before me, "you are quite pale with your vigils: don't you curse me for disturbing your rest?"

"Curse you? No, sir."

"Jane, when will you watch with me again?"

"Whenever I can be useful, sir."

"For instance, the night before I am married! I am sure I shall not be able to sleep. Will you promise to sit up with me to bear me company? To you I can talk of my lovely one: for now you have seen her and know her."

"Yes, sir."

"She's a rare one, is she not, Jane?"

"Yes, sir."

"A strapper—a real strapper, Jane: big, brown, and buxom; with hair just such as the ladies of Carthage must have had. Bless me! there's Dent and Lynn in the stables! Go in by the shrubbery, through that wicket."

[[This conversation was interrupted by activity at the stable. Jane was called away to visit with her aunt who mistreated her and who was gravely ill. She went to confer with Mr. Rochester.]]

I approached the master where he stood at Miss Ingram's side. She turned as I drew near, and looked at me haughtily: her eyes seemed to demand, "What can the creeping creature want now?" and when I said, in a low voice, "Mr. Rochester," she made a movement as if tempted to order me away. I remember her appearance at the moment—it was very graceful and very striking: she wore a morning robe of sky blue crape; a gauzy azure scarf was twisted in her hair. She had been all animation with the game, and irritated pride did not lower the expression of her haughty lineaments.

"Does that person want you?" she inquired of Mr. Rochester; and Mr. Rochester turned to see who the "person" was. He made a curious grimace— one of his strange and equivocal demonstrations—threw down his cue and followed me from the room.

"Well, Jane?" he said, as he rested his back against the schoolroom door, which he had shut.

"If you please, sir, I want leave of absence for a week or two."

[[Mr. Rochester seemed reluctant for Jane to go but offered her some money for her trip. Jane declined the offer.]]

"Mr. Rochester, I may as well mention another matter of business to you while I have the opportunity."

"Matter of business? I am curious to hear it."

"You have as good as informed me, sir, that you are going shortly to be married?"

"Yes; what then?"

"In that case, sir, Adele ought to go to school: I am sure you will perceive the necessity of it."

"To get her out of my bride's way, who might otherwise walk over her rather too emphatically? There's sense in the suggestion; not a doubt of it. Adele, as you say, must go to school; and you, of course, must march straight to—the devil?"

"I hope not, sir; but I must seek another situation somewhere."

"In course!" he exclaimed, with a twang of voice and a distortion of features.

[[Jane left under the impression that Mr. Rochester and Miss Ingram were to marry. It was heavy on her heart that she would need to find a new position. Jane ended up staying away a month, with the aunt passing away and her mean dysfunctional relatives somewhat reconciling with her. Jane returned to Thornfield Hall.]]

I see the narrow stile with stone steps; and I see—Mr. Rochester sitting there, a book and a pencil in his hand; he is writing.

Well, he is not a ghost; yet every nerve I have is unstrung: for a moment I am beyond my own mastery. What does it mean? I did not think I should tremble in this way when I saw him, or lose my voice or the power of motion in his presence. I will go back as soon as I can stir: I need not make an absolute fool of myself. I know another way to the house. However, he has seen me.

"Hillo!" he cries; and he puts up his book and his pencil. "There you are! Come on, if you please."

"And this is Jane Eyre? Are you coming from Millcote, and on foot? Yes—just one of your tricks: not to send for a carriage, and come clattering over street and road like a common mortal, but to steal into your home along with twilight, just as if you were a dream or a shade. What the deuce have you done with yourself this last month?"

"I have been with my aunt, sir, who is dead."

"A true Janian reply! She comes from the other world—from the abode of people who are dead; and tells me so when she meets me alone here in the gloaming! If I dared, I'd touch you, to see if you are substance or shadow, you elf!. Absent from me a whole month, and forgetting me!"

I knew there would be pleasure in meeting my master again, even though broken by the fear that he was so soon to cease to be my master, and by the knowledge that I was nothing to him: but there was ever in Mr. Rochester such a wealth of the power of communicating happiness, that to taste but of the crumbs he scattered to stray and stranger birds like me, was to feast. His last words were balm: they seemed to imply that it imported something to him whether I forgot him or not. And he had spoken of Thornfield as my home— would that it were my home!

I inquired soon if he had not been to London.

"Yes; I suppose you found that out by second sight."

"Mrs. Fairfax told me in a letter."

"And did she inform you what I went to do?"

"Oh, yes, sir! Everybody knew your errand."

"You must see the carriage, Jane, and tell me if you don't think it will suit Mrs. Rochester exactly; and whether she won't look like Queen Boadicea, leaning back against those purple cushions. I wish, Jane, I were a trifle better adapted to match with her externally. Tell me now, fairy as you are— can't you give me a charm to make me a handsome man?"

"It would be past the power of magic, sir;" and, in thought, I added, "A loving eye is all the charm needed: to such you are handsome enough; or rather your sternness has a power beyond beauty."

Mr. Rochester had sometimes read my unspoken thoughts with an acumen to me incomprehensible: in the present instance he took no notice of my abrupt vocal response; but he smiled at me with a certain smile he had of his own, and which he used but on rare occasions. It was the real sunshine of feeling—he shed it over me now.

"Pass, Jane," said he, making room for me to cross the stile: "go up home, and stay your weary little wandering feet at a friend's threshold."

All I had now to do was to obey him in silence: no need for me to colloquies further. I got over the stile without a word, and meant to leave him calmly. An impulse held me fast—a force turned me round. I said—or something in me said for me, and in spite of me—

"Thank you, Mr. Rochester, for your great kindness. I am strangely glad to get back again to you: and wherever you are is my home—my only home."

I walked on so fast that even he could hardly have overtaken me had he tried.

[[Jane wondered about the nuptials of Mr. Rochester and Miss Ingram and tried to deal with her grief .]]

A fortnight of dubious calm succeeded my return to Thornfield Hall. Nothing was said of the master's marriage, and I saw no preparation going on for such an event. Almost every day I asked Mrs. Fairfax if she had yet heard anything decided: her answer was always in the negative. Once she said she had actually put the question to Mr. Rochester as to when he was going to bring his bride home; but he had answered her only by a joke and one of his queer looks, and she could not tell what to make of him.

One thing specially surprised me, and that was, there were no journeyings backward and forward, no visits to Ingram Park: to be sure it was twenty miles off, on the borders of another county; but what was that distance to an ardent lover? To so practiced and indefatigable a horseman as Mr. Rochester, it would be but a morning's ride. I began to cherish hopes I had no right to conceive:

that the match was broken off; that rumor had been mistaken; that one or both parties had changed their minds. I used to look at my master's face to see if it were sad or fierce; but I could not remember the time when it had been so uniformly clear of clouds or evil feelings. If, in the moments I and my pupil spent with him, I lacked spirits and sank into inevitable dejection, he became even gay. Never had he called me more frequently to his presence; never been kinder to me when there—and, alas! never had I loved him so well.

[[One evening when Adele had retired, Jane went to the garden.]]

It was now the sweetest hour of the twenty-four:—"Day its fervid fires had wasted," and dew fell cool on panting plain and scorched summit. Where the sun had gone down in simple state—pure of the pomp of clouds—spread a solemn purple, burning with the light of red jewel and furnace flame at one point, on one hill peak, and extending high and wide, soft and still softer, over half heaven. The east had its own charm or fine deep blue, and its own modest gem, a solitary star: soon it would boast the moon; but she was yet beneath the horizon.

[[Jane realized that Mr. Rochester was in the garden and sought to avoid his notice. Mr. Rochester said quietly –]]

"Jane, come and look at this fellow." I had made no noise: he had not eyes behind—could his shadow feel? I started at first, and then I approached him.

"Look at his wings," said he, "he reminds me rather of a West Indian insect; one does not often see so large and gay a night rover in England; there! he is flown."

The moth roamed away. I was sheepishly retreating also; but Mr. Rochester followed me, and when we reached the wicket, he said—

"Turn back: on so lovely a night it is a shame to sit in the house; and surely no one can wish to go to bed while sunset is thus at meeting with moonrise."

I did not like to walk at this hour alone with Mr. Rochester in the shadowy orchard; but I could not find a reason to allege for leaving him. I followed with lagging step, and thoughts busily bent on discovering a means of extrication; but he himself looked so composed and so grave also, I became ashamed of feeling any confusion: the evil—if evil existent or prospective there was—seemed to lie with me only; his mind was unconscious and quiet.

"Jane," he recommenced, as we entered the laurel walk, and slowly strayed down in the direction of the sunk fence and the horse chestnut, "Thornfield is a pleasant place in summer, is it not?"

"Yes, sir."

"You must have become in some degree attached to the house,—you, who have an eye for natural beauties."

"I am attached to it, indeed."

"And though I don't comprehend how it is, I perceive you have acquired a degree of regard for that foolish little child Adele, too; and even for simple Fairfax?"

"Yes, sir; in different ways, I have an affection for both."

"And would be sorry to part with them?"

"Yes."

"Pity!" he said, and sighed and paused. "It is always the way of events in this life," he continued presently: "no sooner have you got settled in a pleasant resting place, than a voice calls out to you to rise and move on, for the hour of repose is expired."

"Must I move on, sir?" I asked. "Must I leave Thornfield?"

"I believe you must, Jane. I am sorry, Jane, but I believe indeed you must."

This was a blow: but I did not let it prostrate me. "Well, sir, I shall be ready when the order to march comes."

"It is come now—I must give it tonight."

"Then you ARE going to be married, sir?"

"Ex-act-ly—pre-cise-ly: with your usual acuteness, you have hit the nail straight on the head."

"Soon, sir?"

"Very soon, my—that is, Miss Eyre: and you'll remember, Jane, the first time I, or Rumor, plainly intimated to you that it was my intention to put my old bachelor's neck into the sacred noose, to enter into the holy estate of matrimony—to take Miss Ingram in my arms, in short (she's an extensive armful: but that's not to the point—one can't have too much of such a very excellent thing as my beautiful Blanche): well, as I was saying—listen to me, Jane! You're not turning your head to look after more moths, are you? That was only a lady clock, child, 'flying away home.'

"I wish to remind you that it was you who first said to me, with that discretion I respect in you—with that foresight, prudence, and humility which befit your responsible and dependent position—that in case I married Miss Ingram, both you and little Adele had better trot forthwith. I pass over the sort of slur conveyed in this suggestion on the character of my beloved; indeed, when you are far away, Jane, I'll try to forget it: I shall notice only its wisdom. Adele must go to school; and you, Miss Eyre, must get a new situation."

"Yes, sir, I will advertise immediately: and meantime, I suppose—" I was going to say, "I suppose I may stay here, till I find another shelter to betake myself to:" but I stopped, feeling it would not do to risk a long sentence, for my voice was not quite under command.

"In about a month I hope to be a bridegroom," continued Mr. Rochester; "and in the interim, I shall myself look out for employment and an asylum for you."

"Thank you, sir; I am sorry to give—"

"Oh, no need to apologize! I consider that when a dependent does her duty as well as you have done yours, she has a sort of claim upon her employer for any little assistance he can conveniently render her; indeed I have already, through my future mother-in-law, heard of a place that I think will suit: it is to undertake the education of the five daughters of Mrs. Dionysius O'Gall of Bitternutt Lodge, Connaught, Ireland. You'll like Ireland, I think: they're such warm hearted people there, they say."

"It is a long way off, sir."

"No matter—a girl of your sense will not object to the voyage or the distance."

"Not the voyage, but the distance: and then the sea is a barrier—"

"From what, Jane?"

"From England and from Thornfield: and—"

"Well?"

"From YOU, sir." I said this almost involuntarily, and, with as little sanction of free will, my tears gushed out. I did not cry so as to be heard, however; I avoided sobbing. The thought of Ireland struck cold to my heart; and colder the thought of all the brine and foam, destined, as it seemed, to rush between me and the master at whose side I now walked, and coldest the remembrance of the wider ocean—wealth, caste, custom intervened between me and what I naturally and inevitably loved.

"It is a long way," I again said.

"It is, to be sure; and when you get to Ireland, I shall never see you again, Jane: that's morally certain. I never go over to Ireland. We have been good friends, Jane; have we not?"

"Yes, sir."

"And when friends are on the eve of separation, they like to spend the little time that remains to them close to each other. Come! we'll talk over the voyage and the parting quietly while the stars enter into their shining life up in heaven yonder: here is the chestnut tree: here is the bench at its old roots. Come, we will sit there in peace tonight, though we should never more be destined to sit there together." He seated me and himself.

"It is a long way to Ireland, Jane, and I am sorry to send my little friend on such weary travels: but if I can't do better, how is it to be helped? Are you anything akin to me, do you think, Jane?"

I could risk no sort of answer by this time: my heart was still.

"Because," he said, "I sometimes have a queer feeling with regard to you—especially when you are near me, as now: it is as if I had a string somewhere under my left ribs, tightly and inextricably knotted to a similar string situated in the corresponding quarter of your little frame. And if that boisterous Channel, and two hundred miles or so of land come broad between us, I am afraid that cord of communion will be snapped; and then I've a nervous notion I should take to bleeding inwardly. As for you,—you"d forget me."

"That I NEVER should, sir: you know—" Impossible to proceed.

"Jane, do you hear that nightingale singing in the wood? Listen!"

In listening, I sobbed convulsively; for I could repress what I endured no longer; I was obliged to yield, and I was shaken from head to foot with acute distress. When I did speak, it was only to express an impetuous wish that I had never been born, or never come to Thornfield.

"Because you are sorry to leave it?" The vehemence of emotion, stirred by grief and love within me, was claiming mastery, and struggling for full sway, and asserting a right to predominate, to overcome, to live, rise, and reign at last: yes,—and to speak.

"I grieve to leave Thornfield: I love Thornfield:- I love it, because I have lived in it a full and delightful life,—momentarily at least. I have not been trampled on. I have not been petrified. I have not been buried with inferior minds, and excluded from every glimpse of communion with what is bright and energetic and high. I have talked, face to face, with what I reverence, with what I delight in,—with an original, a vigorous, an expanded mind. I have known you, Mr. Rochester; and it strikes me with terror and anguish to feel I absolutely must be torn from you for ever. I see the necessity of departure; and it is like looking on the necessity of death."

"Where do you see the necessity?" he asked suddenly.

"Where? You, sir, have placed it before me."

"In what shape?"

"In the shape of Miss Ingram; a noble and beautiful woman,—your bride."

"My bride! What bride? I have no bride!"

"But you will have."

"Yes;—I will!—I will!" He set his teeth. "Then I must go:- you have said it yourself."

"No: you must stay! I swear it—and the oath shall be kept."

"I tell you I must go!" I retorted, roused to something like passion. "Do you think I can stay to become nothing to you? Do you think I am an automaton?— a machine without feelings? and can bear to have my morsel of bread snatched from my lips, and my drop of living water dashed from my cup? Do you think, because I am poor, obscure, plain, and little, I am soulless and heartless? You think wrong!—I have as much soul as you,—and full as much heart! And if God had gifted me with some beauty and much wealth, I should have made it as hard for you to leave me, as it is now for me to leave you. I am not talking to you now through the medium of custom, conventionalities, nor even of mortal flesh;—it is my spirit that addresses your spirit; just as if we stood at God's feet, equal,—as we are!"

"As we are!" repeated Mr. Rochester—"so," he added, enclosing me in his arms, pressing his lips on my lips: "so, Jane!"

"Yes, so, sir," I rejoined: "and yet not so; for you are a married man—or as good as a married man, and wed to one inferior to you—to one with whom you have no sympathy— whom I do not believe you truly love; for I have seen and heard you sneer at her. I would scorn such a union: therefore I am better than you— let me go!"

"Where, Jane? To Ireland?"

"Yes—to Ireland. I have spoken my mind, and can go anywhere now."

"Jane, be still; don't struggle so, like a wild frantic bird that is rending its own plumage in its desperation."

"I am no bird; and no net ensnares me; I am a free human being with an independent will, which I now exert to leave you."

Another effort set me at liberty, and I stood erect before him.

"And your will shall decide your destiny," he said: "I offer you my hand, my heart, and a share of all my possessions. I ask you to pass through life at my side—to be my second self, and best earthly companion."

A waft of wind came sweeping down the laurel walkway, and trembled through the boughs of the chestnut: it wandered away—away—to an indefinite distance—it died. The nightingale's song was then the only voice of the hour: in listening to it, I again wept. Mr. Rochester sat quiet, looking at me gently and seriously. Some time passed before he spoke; he at last said—

"Come to my side, Jane, and let us explain and understand one another."

"I will never again come to your side: I am torn away now, and cannot return."

"But, Jane, I summon you as my wife: it is you only I intend to marry."

I was silent: I thought he mocked me. "Come, Jane—come hither."

"Your bride stands between us."

He rose, and with a stride reached me.

"My bride is here," he said, again drawing me to him, "because my equal is here, and my likeness. Jane, will you marry me?"

Still I did not answer, and still I writhed myself from his grasp: for I was still incredulous.

"Do you doubt me, Jane?"

"Entirely."

"You have no faith in me?"

"Not a whit."

"Am I a liar in your eyes?" he asked passionately. "Little skeptic, you SHALL be convinced. What love have I for Miss Ingram? None: and that you know. What love has she for me? None: as I have taken pains to prove: I caused a rumor to reach her that my fortune was not a third of what was supposed, and after that I presented myself to see the result; it was coldness both from her and her mother. I would not—I could not—marry Miss Ingram. You— you strange, you almost unearthly thing!—I love as my own flesh. You— poor and obscure, and small and plain as you are—I entreat to accept me as a husband."

"What, me!" I cried, beginning to credit his sincerity: "me who have not a friend in the world but you- if you are my friend: not a shilling but what you have given me?"

"You, Jane, I must have you for my own—entirely my own. Will you be mine? Say yes, quickly."

"Mr. Rochester, let me look at your face: turn to the moonlight."

"Why?"

"Because I want to read your countenance—turn!

"There! you will find it scarcely more legible than a crumpled, scratched page. Read on: only make haste, for I suffer."

His face was very much agitated and very much flushed.

"Oh, Jane, you torture me!" he exclaimed. "With that searching and yet faithful and generous look, you torture me!"

"How can I do that? If you are true, and your offer real, my only feelings to you must be gratitude and devotion— they cannot torture."

"Gratitude!" he stated; and added wildly—"Jane accept me quickly. Say, Edward—give me my name—Edward—I will marry you."

"Are you in earnest? Do you truly love me? Do you sincerely wish me to be your wife?"

"I do; and if an oath is necessary to satisfy you, I swear it."

"Then, sir, I will marry you.

"Edward—my little wife!"

"Dear Edward!"

"Come to me—come to me entirely now," said he; and added, in his deepest tone, speaking in my ear as his cheek was laid on mine, "Make my happiness—I will make yours.

"God pardon me!" he subjoined ere long; "and man meddle not with me: I have her, and will hold her."

"There is no one to meddle, sir. I have no kindred to interfere."

"No—that is the best of it," he said. Sitting by him, roused from the nightmare of parting—called to the paradise of union—I thought only of the bliss given me to drink in so abundant a flow. Again and again he said, "Are you happy, Jane?" And again and again I answered, "Yes." After which he murmured, "It will atone —it will atone. Have I not found her friendless, and cold, and comfortless? Will I not guard, and cherish, and solace her? Is there not love in my heart, and constancy in my resolves? It will expiate at God's tribunal. I know my Maker sanctions what I do. For the world's judgment—I wash my hands thereof. For man's opinion—I defy it."

But what had befallen the night? The moon was not yet set, and we were all in shadow: I could scarcely see my master's face, near as I was. And what ailed the chestnut tree? it writhed and groaned; while wind roared in the laurel walk, and came sweeping over us.

"We must go in," said Mr. Rochester: "the weather changes. I could have sat with thee till morning, Jane."

"And so," thought I, "could I with you." I should have said so, perhaps, but a livid, vivid spark leapt out of a cloud at which I was looking, and there was a crack, a crash, and a close rattling peal; and I thought only of hiding my dazzled eyes against Mr. Rochester's shoulder.

The rain rushed down. He hurried me up the walk, through the grounds, and into the house; but we were quite wet before we could pass the threshold. He was taking off my shawl in the hall, and shaking the water out of my loosened hair, when Mrs. Fairfax emerged from her room. I did not observe her at first, nor did Mr. Rochester. The lamp was lit. The clock was on the stroke of twelve.

"Hasten to take off your wet things," said he; "and before you go, goodnight— goodnight, my darling!"

He kissed me repeatedly. When I looked up, on leaving his arms, there stood the widow, pale, grave, and amazed. I only smiled at her, and ran upstairs. "Explanation will do for another time," thought I. Still, when I reached my chamber, I felt a pang at the idea she should even temporarily misconstrue what she had seen. But joy soon effaced every other feeling; and loud as the wind blew, near and deep as the thunder crashed, fierce and frequent as the lightning gleamed, as the rain fell during a storm of two hours' duration, I experienced no fear and little awe. Mr. Rochester came thrice to my door in the course of it, to ask if I was safe and tranquil: and that was comfort, that was strength for anything.

Before I left my bed in the morning, little Adele came running in to tell me that the great horse chestnut   at the bottom of the orchard had been struck by lightning in the night, and half of it split away. As I rose and dressed, I thought over what had happened, and wondered if it were a dream. I could not be certain of the reality till I had seen Mr. Rochester again, and heard him renew his words of love and promise.

While arranging my hair, I looked at my face in the glass, and felt it was no longer plain: there was hope in its aspect and life in its color; and my eyes seemed as if they had beheld the fount of fruition, and borrowed beams from the lustrous ripple. I had often been unwilling to look at my master, because I feared he could not be pleased at my look.

I was not surprised, when I ran down into the hall, to see that a brilliant June morning had succeeded to the tempest of the night; and to feel, through the open glass door, the breathing of a fresh and fragrant breeze. Nature must be gladsome when I was so happy.

I received an embrace and a kiss. It seemed natural: it seemed genial to be so well loved, so caressed by him.

"Jane, you look blooming, and smiling, and pretty," said he: "truly pretty this morning. Is this my pale, little elf? Is this my mustard seed? This little sunny faced girl with the dimpled cheek and rosy lips; the satin smooth hazel hair.

"This morning I wrote to my banker in London to send me certain jewels he has in his keeping,—heirlooms for the ladies of Thornfield. In a day or two I hope to pour them into your lap: for every privilege, every attention shall be yours."

"Oh, sir!—never rain jewels! I don't like to hear them spoken of. Jewels for Jane Eyre sounds unnatural and strange: I would rather not have them. Think of other subjects, and speak of other things. Don't address me as if I were a beauty; I am your plain, Quakerish governess."

"You are a beauty in my eyes, and a beauty just after the desire of my heart,— delicate and aerial. I never met your likeness. Jane, you please me. I am influenced—conquered; and the influence is sweeter than I can express; and the conquest I undergo has a witchery beyond any triumph I can win. Why do you smile, Jane? What does that inexplicable, that uncanny turn of countenance mean?"

"I was thinking, sir, of Hercules and Samson with their charmers—"

"You were, you little elfish—"

"Hush, sir! You don't talk very wisely just now; any more than those gentlemen acted very wisely. However, had they been married, they would no doubt by their severity as husbands have made up for their softness as suitors; and so will you, I fear. I wonder how you will answer me a year hence, should I ask a favor it does not suit your convenience or pleasure to grant."

"Ask me something now, Jane,—the least thing: I desire to be entreated—"

"Indeed I will, sir; I have my petition all ready."

"Speak! But if you look up and smile with that countenance, I shall swear concession before I know to what, and that will make a fool of me."

"Not at all, sir; I ask only this: don't send for the jewels, and don't crown me with roses: you might as well put a border of gold lace round that plain pocket handkerchief you have there."

"I might as well 'gild refined gold.' I know it: you request is granted then—for the time. I will remand the order I dispatched to my banker. But you have not yet asked for anything; you have prayed a gift to be withdrawn: try again."

"Well then, sir, have the goodness to gratify my curiosity, which is much piqued on one point."

He looked disturbed. "What? what?" he said hastily. "Curiosity is a dangerous petition."

"Now, King Ahasuerus! What do I want with half your estate? Do you think I am a Jew usurer, seeking good investment in land? I would much rather have all your confidence. You will not exclude me from your confidence if you admit me to your heart?"

"Why did you take such pains to make me believe you wished to marry Miss

Ingram?"

"Well, I feigned courtship of Miss Ingram, because I wished to render you as madly in love with me as I was with you; and I knew jealousy would be the best ally I could call in for the furtherance of that end."

Smiling at me, he stroked my hair. "I think I may confess," he continued, "even although I should make you a little indignant, Jane—and I have seen what a fire spirit you can be when you are indignant. You glowed in the cool moonlight last night, when you mutinied against fate, and claimed your rank as my equal. Jane, it was you who made me the offer."

"Of course I did. But to the point if you please, sir—Miss Ingram?"

"She, on the contrary, deserted me: the idea of my insolvency cooled, or rather extinguished, her flame in a moment."

I loved him very much—more than I could trust myself to say—more than words had power to express. My future husband was becoming to me my whole world; and more than the world: almost my hope of heaven. He stood between me and every thought of religion, as an eclipse intervenes between man and the broad sun. I could not, in those days, see God for His creature: of whom I had made an idol.

[[Jane wished to continue in their protocol and roles until their wedding in a month. The night before the wedding, Mr. Rochester away on business, returned to find Jane anxiously waiting for him.]]

"Take a seat and bear me company, Jane: please God, it is the last meal but one you will eat at Thornfield Hall for a long time."

I sat down near him, but told him I could not eat. "Is it because you have the prospect of a journey before you, Jane? Is it the thoughts of going to London that takes away your appetite?"

"I cannot see my prospects clearly tonight, sir; and I hardly know what thoughts I have in my head. Everything in life seems unreal."

"Except me: I am substantial enough—touch me."

"You, sir, are the most phantom like of all: you are a mere dream."

"Yes; though I touch it, it is a dream," said I, as I put it down from before my face. "Sir, have you finished supper?"

"Yes, Jane." I rang the bell and ordered away the tray. When we were again alone, I stirred the fire, and then took a low seat at my master's knee.

"It is near midnight," I said. "Yes: but remember, Jane, you promised to wake with me the night before my wedding."

"I did; and I will keep my promise, for an hour or two at least: I have no wish to go to bed."

"Are all your arrangements complete?"

"All, sir."

"And on my part likewise," he returned, "I have settled everything; and we shall leave Thornfield tomorrow, shortly after our return from church."

[[Jane had unsettling dreams that she shared with Mr. Rochester. She told him that she saw a crazed woman in her room two nights before the wedding.]]

"On waking, a gleam dazzled my eyes. There was a candlelight on the dressing-table, and the door of the closet, where, before going to bed, I had hung my wedding-dress and veil, stood open; I heard a rustling there. I asked, 'Sophie, what are you doing?' No one answered; but a form emerged from the closet; it took the light, held it aloft, and surveyed the garments. 'Sophie! Sophie!' I again cried: and still it was silent. Bewilderment, came over me. Mr. Rochester, this was not Sophie, it was not Leah, it was not Mrs. Fairfax: it was not—no, I was sure of it, and am still—it was not even that strange woman, Grace Poole."

"It must have been one of them," interrupted my master.

"No, sir, I solemnly assure you to the contrary. The shape standing before me had never crossed my eyes within the precincts of Thornfield Hall before; the height, the contour were new to me."

"Describe it, Jane."

"It seemed, sir, a woman, tall and large, with thick and dark hair hanging long down her back. I know not what dress she had on: it was white and straight."

"Did you see her face?"

"Not at first. But presently she took my veil from its place; she held it up, gazed at it long, and then she threw it over her own head, and turned to the mirror. At that moment I her reflection."

"And how were they?"

"Fearful and ghastly to me—oh, sir, I never saw a face like it! It was a discoloured face—it was a savage face, the black eyebrows widely raised over the bloodshot eyes."

"Ah!—what did it do?"

"Sir, it removed my veil from its gaunt head, rent it in two parts, and flinging both on the floor, trampled on them."

"Afterwards?"

"It drew aside the window-curtain and looked out; perhaps it saw dawn approaching, for, taking the candle, it retreated to the door. Just at my bedside, the figure stopped: the fiery eyes glared upon me—she thrust up her candle close to my face, and extinguished it under my eyes. I lost consciousness. I became insensible from terror."

"Who was with you when you revived?"

"No one, sir, but the broad day. I felt that though enfeebled I was not ill, and determined that to none but you would I impart this vision. Now, sir, tell me who and what that woman was?"

"The creature of an over-stimulated brain; that is certain. I must be careful of you, my treasure: nerves like yours were not made for rough handling."

"Sir, depend on it, my nerves were not in fault; the thing was real: the transaction actually took place."

"The day is already commenced which is to bind us indissolubly; and when we are once united, there shall be no recurrence of these mental terrors: I guarantee that."

"Mental terrors, sir! I wish I could believe them to be only such: I wish it more now than ever; since even you cannot explain to me the mystery of that awful visitant."

"And since I cannot do it, Jane, it must have been unreal."

"But, sir, when I said so to myself on rising this morning, and when I looked round the room to gather courage and comfort from the cheerful aspect of each familiar object in full daylight, there—on the carpet—I saw what gave the distinct lie to my hypothesis,—the veil, torn from top to bottom in two halves!"

I felt Mr. Rochester start and shudder; he hastily flung his arms round me. "Thank God!" he exclaimed, "that if anything malignant did come near you last night, it was only the veil that was harmed. Oh, to think what might have happened!"

He drew his breath short, and strained me so close to him, I could scarcely pant. After some minutes' silence, he continued—

"Now, Jane, I'll explain to you all about it. It was half dream, half reality. A woman did, I doubt not, enter your room: and that woman was—must have been—Grace Poole. You call her a strange being yourself: from all you know, you have reason so to call her—what did she do to me? what to Mason.

"In a state between sleeping and waking, you noticed her entrance and her actions; but feverish, almost delirious as you were, you ascribed to her a goblin appearance different from her own: the long disheveled hair, the swelled face, the exaggerated stature, were figments of imagination; results of nightmare: the spiteful tearing of the veil was real: and it is like her.

"I see you would ask why I keep such a woman in my house: when we have been married a year and a day, I will tell you; but not now. Are you satisfied, Jane? Do you accept my solution of the mystery?"

I reflected, and in truth it appeared to me the only possible one: satisfied I was not, but to please him I endeavored to appear so— relieved, I certainly did feel; so I answered him with a contented smile. And now, as it was long past one, I prepared to leave him.

[[The wedding morning –]]

There were no groomsmen, no bridesmaids, no relatives, none but Mr. Rochester and I. Our place was taken at the communion rails. Hearing a cautious step behind me, I glanced over my shoulder: one of the strangers—a gentleman, evidently—was advancing up the chancel. The service began. The explanation of the intent of matrimony was gone through; and then the clergyman came a step further forward, and, bending slightly towards Mr. Rochester, went on.

"I require and charge you both (as ye will answer at the dreadful day of judgment, when the secrets of all hearts shall be disclosed), that if either of you know any impediment why ye may not lawfully be joined together in matrimony, ye do now confess it; for be ye well assured that so many as are coupled together otherwise than God's Word doth allow, are not joined together by God, neither is their matrimony lawful."

He paused, as the custom is. When is the pause after that sentence ever broken by reply? Not, perhaps, once in a hundred years. And the clergyman, who had not lifted his eyes from his book, and had held his breath but for a moment, was proceeding to ask, "Wilt thou have this woman for thy wedded wife?"—when a distinct and near voice said—

"The marriage cannot go on: I declare the existence of an impediment."

The clergyman looked up at the speaker and stood mute; the clerk did the same; Mr. Rochester moved slightly, as if an earthquake had rolled under his feet: taking a firmer footing, and not turning his head or eyes, he said, "Proceed."

Profound silence fell when he had uttered that word, with deep but low intonation. Presently Mr. Wood said—

"I cannot proceed without some investigation into what has been asserted, and evidence of its truth or falsehood."

"The ceremony is quite broken off," subjoined the voice behind us. "I am in a condition to prove my allegation: an insuperable impediment to this marriage exists."

Mr. Rochester heard, but heeded not: he stood stubborn and rigid, making no movement but to possess himself of my hand. What a hot and strong grasp he had! How his eyes shone, still watchful, and yet wild beneath!

Mr. Wood seemed at a loss. "What is the nature of the impediment?" he asked. "Perhaps it may be got over—explained away?"

The speaker came forward and leaned on the rails. He continued, uttering each word distinctly, calmly, steadily, but not loudly—

"It consists in the existence of a previous marriage. Mr. Rochester has a wife now living."

My nerves vibrated to those low spoken words as they had never vibrated to thunder—my blood felt their subtle violence as it had never felt frost or fire; but I was collected, and in no danger of swooning. I looked at Mr. Rochester: I made him look at me. His whole face was colorless rock: his eye was both spark and flint. He disavowed nothing: he seemed as if he would defy all things. Without speaking, without smiling, without seeming to recognize in me a human being, he only twined my waist with his arm and riveted me to his side.

"Who are you?" he asked of the intruder. "My name is Briggs, a solicitor. "And you would thrust on me a wife?"

"I would remind you of your lady's existence, sir, which the law recognizes, if you do not."

"Favor me with an account of her—with her name, her parentage, her place of abode."

"Certainly." Mr. Briggs calmly took a paper from his pocket, and read out in a sort of official, nasal voice:-

Mr. Rochester, on hearing the name, set his teeth; he experienced, too, a sort of strong convulsive quiver; near to him as I was, I felt the spasmodic movement of fury or despair run through his frame. The second stranger, who had hitherto lingered in the background, now drew near; a pale face looked over the solicitor's shoulder—yes, it was Mason himself. Mr. Rochester turned and glared at him. "What have YOU to say?"

An inaudible reply escaped Mason's white lips.

"The devil is in it if you cannot answer distinctly. I again demand, what have you to say?"

"Sir—sir," interrupted the clergyman, "do not forget you are in a sacred place." Then addressing Mason, he inquired gently, "Are you aware, sir, whether or not this gentleman's wife is still living?"

"She is now living at Thornfield Hall," said Mason. "I saw her there last April. I am her brother."

"At Thornfield Hall!" cried the clergyman. "Impossible! I am an old resident in this neighborhood, sir, and I never heard of a Mrs. Rochester at Thornfield Hall."

Mr. Rochester muttered, "No, by God! I took care that none should hear of it—or of her under that name." He mused—for ten minutes he held counsel with himself: he formed his resolve, and announced, "Enough! There will be no wedding today."

Mr. Rochester continued, hardily and recklessly: "Bigamy is an ugly word!—I meant, however, to be a bigamist; but fate has out maneuvered me, or Providence has checked me,—perhaps the last. I am little better than a devil at this moment; and, as my pastor there would tell me, deserve no doubt the sternest judgments of God, even to the quenchless fire and deathless worm. Gentlemen, my plan is broken up.

"What this lawyer and his client say is true: I have been married, and the woman to whom I was married lives! You say you never heard of a Mrs. Rochester at the house up yonder, Wood; but I daresay you have many a time inclined your ear to gossip about the mysterious lunatic kept there under watch and ward. Some have whispered to you that she is my bastard half sister: some, my cast off mistress. I now inform you that she is my wife, whom I married fifteen years ago,—Bertha Mason by name; sister of this resolute personage.

"Bertha Mason is mad; and she came of a mad family; idiots and maniacs through three generations? Her mother, the Creole, was both a madwoman and a drunkard!—as I found out after I had wed the daughter: for they were silent on family secrets before. Bertha, like a dutiful child, copied her parent in both points.

"But I owe you no further explanation. Briggs, Wood, Mason, I invite you all to come up to the house and visit Mrs. Poole's patient, and MY WIFE! You shall see what sort of a being I was cheated into espousing, and judge whether or not I had a right to break the compact, and seek sympathy with something at least human. This girl," he continued, looking at me, "knew no more than you, Wood, of the disgusting secret: she thought all was fair and legal and never dreamt she was going to be entrapped into a feigned union with a defrauded wretch, already bound to a bad, mad, and embruted partner! Come all of you—follow!"

[[They all made haste by carriage to Thornfield Manor]]

We mounted the first staircase, passed up the gallery, proceeded to the third story: the low, black door, admitted us to the tapestried room, with its great bed and its pictorial cabinet.

"You know this place, Mason," said our guide; "she bit and stabbed you here."

He lifted the hangings from the wall, uncovering the second door: this, too, he opened. In a room without a window, there burnt a fire. Grace Poole bent over the fire, apparently cooking something in a saucepan. In the deep shade, at the farther end of the room, a figure ran backwards and forwards. What it was, whether beast or human being, one could not, at first sight, tell: it grovelled, seemingly, on all fours; it snatched and growled like some strange wild animal: but it was covered with clothing, and a quantity of dark, grizzled hair, wild as a mane, hid its head and face.

"Mrs. Poole!" said Mr. Rochester. "How are you? and how is your charge today?"

"We're tolerable, sir, I thank you," replied Grace, "rather snappish, but not rageous."

A fierce cry seemed to give the lie to her favorable report: the clothed hyena rose up, and stood tall.

"Ah! sir, she sees you!" exclaimed Grace: "you"d better not stay."

"Only a few moments, Grace: you must allow me a few moments."

The maniac bellowed: she parted her shaggy locks from her visage, and gazed wildly at her visitors. I recognized well that purple face,—those bloated features. Mrs. Poole advanced.

"Keep out of the way," said Mr. Rochester, thrusting her aside: "she has no knife now, I suppose, and I'm on my guard."

"One never knows what she has, sir: she is so cunning."

"We had better leave her," whispered Mason.

"Go to the devil!" was his brother-in-law's recommendation.

The three gentlemen retreated simultaneously. Mr. Rochester flung me behind him: the lunatic sprang and grappled his throat viciously, and laid her teeth to his cheek: they struggled. She was a big woman, in stature almost equaling her husband. She showed virile force in the contest—more than once she almost throttled him, athletic as he was.

He could have settled her with a well planted blow; but he would not strike: he would only wrestle. At last he mastered her arms; Grace Poole gave him a cord, and he pinioned them behind her: with more rope, which was at hand, he bound her to a chair. The operation was performed amidst the fiercest yells and the most convulsive plunges. Mr. Rochester then turned to the spectators.

"That is MY WIFE," said he. "Such is the sole conjugal embrace I am ever to know—such are the endearments which are to solace my leisure hours! And THIS is what I wished to have" (laying his hand on my shoulder): "this young girl, who stands so grave and quiet at the mouth of hell, looking collectedly at the gambols of a demon. Wood and Briggs, look at the difference! Compare these clear eyes, this face with that mask; then judge me, priest of the gospel and man of the law, and remember with what judgment ye judge ye shall be judged! Off with you now."

We all withdrew. Mr. Rochester stayed a moment behind us, to give some further order to Grace Poole. I stood at the half open door of my own room, to which I had now withdrawn. The house cleared, I shut myself in, fastened the bolt that none might intrude, and proceeded—not to weep, not to mourn, I was yet too calm for that, but—mechanically to take off the wedding dress, and replace it with the gown I had worn yesterday, as I thought, for the last time. I then sat down: I felt weak and tired.

The morning had been a quiet morning enough—all except the brief scene with the lunatic: the transaction in the church had not been noisy; there was no explosion of passion, no loud altercation, no dispute, no defiance or challenge, no tears, no sobs: a few words had been spoken, a calmly pronounced objection to the marriage made; some stern, short questions put by Mr. Rochester; answers, explanations given, evidence adduced; an open admission of the truth had been uttered by my master; then the living proof had been seen; the intruders were gone, and all was over.

I was in my own room as usual—just myself, without obvious change: nothing had smitten me or scathed me. And yet where was the Jane Eyre of yesterday? —where was her life?—where were her prospects? Jane Eyre, who had been an ardent, expectant woman—almost a bride, was a cold, solitary girl again: her life was pale; her prospects were desolate.

Mr. Rochester was not to me what he had been; for he was not what I had thought him. I would not ascribe vice to him; I would not say he had betrayed me; but the attribute of stainless truth was gone from his idea, and from his presence I must go: THAT I perceived well.

My eyes were covered and closed: eddying darkness seemed to swim round me, and reflection came in as black and confused a flow. Self abandoned, relaxed, and effortless, I seemed to have laid me down in the dried up bed of a great river; I heard a flood loosened in remote mountains, and felt the torrent come: to rise I had no will, to flee I had no strength.

That bitter hour cannot be described: in truth, "the waters came into my soul; I sank in deep mire; I came into deep waters; the floods overflowed me."

Some time in the afternoon I raised my head, and looking round and seeing the western sun gilding the sign of its decline on the wall, I asked, "What am I to do?"

But the answer my mind gave—"Leave Thornfield at once"

[[As Jane left her room she saw that Mr. Rochester was sitting in a chair near her door.]]

"You come out at last," he said. "Well, I have been waiting for you long, and listening: yet not one movement have I heard, nor one sob: five minutes more of that death like hush, and I should have forced the lock. So you shun me?— you shut yourself up and grieve alone! I would rather you had come and upbraided me with vehemence. You are passionate. I expected a scene of some kind. I was prepared for the hot rain of tears; only I wanted them to be shed on me. But I err: you have not wept at all! No trace of tears.

"Well, Jane! not a word of reproach? Nothing bitter? Nothing to cut a feeling or sting a passion? You sit quietly where I have placed you, and regard me with a weary, passive look."

"Jane, I never meant to wound you thus. Will you ever forgive me?"

Reader, I forgave him at the moment and on the spot. There was such deep remorse in his eye, such true pity in his tone, such manly energy in his manner; and besides, there was such unchanged love in his whole look and mien—I forgave him all: yet not in words, not outwardly; only at my heart's core.

"You know I am a scoundrel, Jane?" ere long he inquired wistfully— wondering, I suppose, at my continued silence, the result rather of weakness than of will.

"Yes, sir."

"Then tell me so roundly and sharply—don't spare me."

"I cannot: I am tired and sick. I want some water." He heaved a sort of shuddering sigh, and taking me in his arms, carried me downstairs. He put wine to my lips; I tasted it and revived; then I ate something he offered me, and was soon myself. He was quite near. "If I could go out of life now, without too sharp a pang, it would be well for me. I must leave him, it appears. I do not want to leave him—I cannot leave him."

"How are you now, Jane?"

"Much better, sir; I shall be well soon."

"Taste the wine again, Jane." He looked at me attentively. Suddenly he turned away, with an inarticulate exclamation, full of passionate emotion of some kind; he walked fast through the room and came back; he stooped towards me as if to kiss me; but I remembered caresses were now forbidden. I turned my face away and put his aside.

"What!—How is this?" he exclaimed hastily. "Oh, I know! you won't kiss the husband of Bertha Mason?

"At any rate, there is neither room nor claim for me, sir."

"Why, Jane? I will spare you the trouble of much talking; I will answer for you— Because I have a wife already, you would reply.—I guess rightly?"

"Yes."

"If you think so, you must have a strange opinion of me; you must regard me as a base and low rake who has been simulating disinterested love in order to draw you into a snare deliberately laid, and strip you of honor and rob you of self respect. What do you say to that? I see you can say nothing in the first place, you are faint still, and have enough to do to draw your breath; in the second place, you cannot yet accustom yourself to accuse and revile me, and besides, the flood gates of tears are opened, and they would rush out if you spoke much; and you have no desire to expostulate, to upbraid, to make a scene: you are thinking how TO ACT—TALKING you consider is of no use. I know you."

"Sir, I do not wish to act against you," I said; and my unsteady voice warned me to curtail my sentence.

"You have as good as said that I am a married man—as a married man you will shun me, keep out of my way: just now you have refused to kiss me. You intend to make yourself a complete stranger to me: to live under this roof only as Adele's governess; if ever I say a friendly word to you, if ever a friendly feeling inclines you again to me, you will say,—"That man had nearly made me his mistress: I must be ice and rock to him;" and ice and rock you will accordingly become."

I cleared and steadied my voice to reply: "All is changed about me, sir; I must change too—there is no doubt of that; and to avoid fluctuations of feeling, and continual combats with recollections and associations, there is only one way— Adele must have a new governess, sir."

"Oh, Adele will go to school—I have settled that already; nor do I mean to torment you with the hideous associations and recollections of Thornfield Hall —this accursed place, his insolent vault, offering the ghastliness of living death to the light of the open sky—this narrow stone hell, with its one real fiend, worse than a legion of such as we imagine. Jane, you shall not stay here, nor will I. I was wrong ever to bring you to Thornfield Hall, knowing as I did how it was haunted.

"I charged them to conceal from you, before I ever saw you, all knowledge of the curse of the place; merely because I feared Adele never would have a governess to stay if she knew with what inmate she was housed, and my plans would not permit me to remove the maniac elsewhere—though I possess an old house, Ferndean Manor, even more retired and hidden than this, where I could have lodged her safely enough, had not a scruple about the unhealthiness of the situation, in the heart of a wood, made my conscience recoil from the arrangement. Probably those damp walls would soon have eased me of her charge: but to each villain his own vice; and mine is not a tendency to indirect assassination, even of what I most hate.

"I'll shut up Thornfield Hall: I'll nail up the front door and board the lower windows: I'll give Mrs. Poole two hundred a year to live here with MY WIFE, as you term that fearful hag: Grace will do much for money, and she shall have her son to bear her company and be at hand to give her aid in the paroxysms, when MY WIFE is prompted by her familiar to burn people in their beds at night, to stab them, and so on—"

"Sir," I interrupted him, "you are inexorable for that unfortunate lady: you speak of her with hate—with vindictive antipathy. It is cruel—she cannot help being mad."

"Jane, my darling, you don't know what you are talking about; you misjudge me again: it is not because she is mad I hate her. If you were mad, do you think I should hate you?"

"I do indeed, sir."

"Then you are mistaken, and you know nothing about me, and nothing about the sort of love of which I am capable. Every atom of your flesh is as dear to me as my own: in pain and sickness it would still be dear. Your mind is my treasure, and if it were broken, it would be my treasure still.

"But why do I follow that train of ideas? I only ask you to endure one more night under this roof, Jane; and then, farewell to its miseries and terrors for ever! I have a place to repair to, which will be a secure sanctuary from hateful reminiscences, from unwelcome intrusion—even from falsehood and slander."

"And take Adele with you, sir," I interrupted; "she will be a companion for you."

"What do you mean, Jane? I told you I would send Adele to school; and what do I want with a child for a companion, and not my own child,—a French dancer's bastard? Why do you importune me about her! I say, why do you assign Adele to me for a companion?"

"You spoke of a retirement, sir; and retirement and solitude are dull: too dull for you."

"Solitude! solitude!" he reiterated with irritation. "I see I must come to an explanation. I don't know what sphinx like expression is forming in your countenance. You are to share my solitude. Do you understand?"

I shook my head: it required a degree of courage, excited as he was becoming, even to risk that mute sign of dissent. He had been walking fast about the room, and he stopped, as if suddenly rooted to one spot. He looked at me long and hard: I turned my eyes from him, fixed them on the fire, and tried to assume and maintain a quiet, collected aspect.

He recommenced his walk, but soon again stopped, and this time just before me.

"Jane! will you hear reason?" His voice was hoarse; his look that of a man who is just about to burst an insufferable bond and plunged headlong into wildness.

I was not afraid: not in the least. I felt an inward power; a sense of influence, which supported me. The crisis was perilous. I took hold of his clenched hand, and said to him, soothingly—

"Sit down; I'll talk to you as long as you like, and hear all you have to say, whether reasonable or unreasonable."

He sat down: but he did not get leave to speak directly. I had been struggling with tears for some time: I had taken great pains to repress them, because I knew he would not like to see me weep. Now, however, I considered it well to let them flow as freely and as long as they liked. So I gave way and cried heartily.

Soon I heard him earnestly entreating me to be composed. I said I could not while he was in such a passion.

"But I am not angry, Jane: I only love you too well; and you had steeled your little pale face with such a resolute, frozen look, I could not endure it. Hush, now, and wipe your eyes."

His softened voice announced that he was subdued; so I, in my turn, became calm. Now he made an effort to rest his head on my shoulder, but I would not permit it. Then he would draw me to him: no.

"Jane! Jane!" he said, in such an accent of bitter sadness it thrilled along every nerve I had; "you don't love me, then? It was only my station, and the rank of my wife, that you valued? Now that you think me disqualified to become your husband, you recoil from my touch as if I were some toad or ape."

These words cut me: yet what could I do or I say? I ought probably to have done or said nothing; but I was so tortured by a sense of remorse at thus hurting his feelings, I could not control the wish to drop balm where I had wounded.

"I DO love you," I said, "more than ever: but I must not show or indulge the feeling: and this is the last time I must express it."

"The last time, Jane! What! do you think you can live with me, and see me daily, and yet, if you still love me, be always cold and distant?"

"No, sir; that I am certain I could not; and therefore I see there is but one way: but you will be furious if I mention it."

"Oh, mention it! If I storm, you have the art of weeping."

"Mr. Rochester, I must leave you."

"For how long, Jane? For a few minutes, while you smooth your hair which is somewhat disheveled; and bathe your face—which looks feverish?"

"I must leave Adele and Thornfield. I must part with you for my whole life: I must begin a new existence among strange faces and strange scenes."

"Of course: I told you you should. I pass over the madness about parting from me. You mean you must become a part of me. As to the new existence, it is all right: you shall yet be my wife: I am not married. You shall be Mrs. Rochester—both virtually and nominally. I shall keep only to you so long as you and I live. You shall go to a place I have in the south of France: a whitewashed villa on the shores of the Mediterranean. There you shall live a happy, and guarded, and most innocent life. Never fear that I wish to lure you into error—to make you my mistress. Why did you shake your head? Jane, you must be reasonable, or in truth I shall again become frantic."

His voice and hand quivered, his eyes glazed. Still I dared to speak.

"Sir, your wife is living: that is a fact acknowledged this morning by yourself. If I lived with you as you desire, I should then be your mistress: to say otherwise is false."

"Jane, I am not a gentle tempered man—you forget that: I am not long enduring; I am not cool and dispassionate.

To agitate him thus deeply, by a resistance he so abhorred, was cruel: to yield was out of the question. I did what human beings do instinctively when they are driven to utter extremity— looked for aid to one higher than man: the words "God help me!" burst involuntarily from my lips.

"I am a fool!" cried Mr. Rochester suddenly. "I keep telling her I am not married, and do not explain to her why. I forget she knows nothing of the character of that woman, or of the circumstances attending my infernal union with her. Can you listen to me?"

"Yes, sir; for hours if you will."

"I ask only minutes. Jane, did you ever hear or know at I was not the eldest son of my house: that I had once a brother older than I?"

"I remember Mrs. Fairfax told me so once.

"And did you ever hear that my father was an avaricious, grasping man?"

"I have understood something to that effect."

"Well, Jane, being so, it was his resolution to keep the property together; he could not bear the idea of dividing his estate and leaving me a fair portion: all, he resolved, should go to my brother, Rowland. Yet as little could he endure that a son of his should be a poor man. I must be provided for by a wealthy marriage. He sought me a partner betimes. Mr. Mason, a West India planter and merchant, was his old acquaintance. He was certain his possessions were real and vast: he made inquiries.

"Mr. Mason, he found, had a son and daughter; and he learned from him that he could and would give the latter a fortune of thirty thousand pounds: that sufficed. When I left college, I was sent out to Jamaica, to espouse a bride already courted for me. My father said nothing about her money; but he told me Miss Mason was the boast of Spanish Town for her beauty: and this was no lie.

I found her a fine woman, in the style of Blanche Ingram: tall, dark, and majestic. Her family wished to secure me because I was of a good race; and so did she. They showed her to me in parties, splendidly dressed. I seldom saw her alone, and had very little private conversation with her. She flattered me, and lavishly displayed for my pleasure her charms and accomplishments.

"All the men in her circle seemed to admire her and envy me. I was dazzled, my senses were excited; and being ignorant, raw, and inexperienced, I thought I loved her. There is no folly so besotted that the idiotic rivalries of society, the rashness, the blindness of youth, will not hurry a man to its commission. Her relatives encouraged me; competitors piqued me; she allured me: a marriage was achieved almost before I knew where I was.

"Oh, I have no respect for myself when I think of that act!—an agony of inward contempt masters me. I never loved, I never esteemed, I did not even know her. I was not sure of the existence of one virtue in her nature: I had marked neither modesty, nor benevolence, nor candor, nor refinement in her mind or manners—and, I married her: gross, grovelling, mole eyed blockhead that I was! With less sin I might have—But let me remember to whom I am speaking."

"My bride's mother I had never seen: I understood she was dead. The honeymoon over, I learned my mistake; she was only mad, and shut up in a lunatic asylum. There was a younger brother, too—a complete dumb idiot. The elder one, whom you have seen (and whom I cannot hate, whilst I abhor all his kindred, because he has some grains of affection in his feeble mind, shown in the continued interest he takes in his wretched sister, and also in a dog like attachment he once bore me), will probably be in the same state one day. My father and my brother Rowland knew all this; but they thought only of the thirty thousand pounds, and joined in the plot against me."

"These were vile discoveries; but except for the treachery of concealment, I should have made them no subject of reproach to my wife, even when I found her nature wholly alien to mine, her tastes obnoxious to me, her cast of mind common, low, narrow, and singularly incapable of being led to anything higher, expanded to anything larger—when I found that I could not pass a single evening, nor even a single hour of the day with her in comfort; that kindly conversation could not be sustained between us, because whatever topic I started, immediately received from her a turn at once coarse and trite, perverse and imbecile—when I perceived that I should never have a quiet or settled household, because no servant would bear the continued outbreaks of her violent and unreasonable temper, or the vexations of her absurd, contradictory, exacting orders—even then I restrained myself: I eschewed upbraiding, I curtailed remonstrance; I tried to bear my repentance and disgust in secret; I repressed the deep antipathy I felt.

"Jane, I will not trouble you with abominable details: some strong words shall express what I have to say. I lived with that woman upstairs four years, and before that time she had tried me indeed: her character ripened and developed with frightful rapidity; her vices sprang up fast and rank: they were so strong, only cruelty could check them, and I would not use cruelty. What a pygmy intellect she had, and what giant propensities! How fearful were the curses those propensities entailed on me! Bertha Mason, the true daughter of an infamous mother, dragged me through all the hideous and degrading agonies which must attend a man bound to a wife at once intemperate and unchaste.

"My brother in the interval was dead, and at the end of the four years my father died too. I was rich enough now—yet poor to hideous indigence: a nature the most gross, impure, depraved I ever saw, was associated with mine, and called by the law and by society a part of me. And I could not rid myself of it by any legal proceedings: for the doctors now discovered that MY WIFE was mad— her excesses had prematurely developed the germs of insanity. Jane, you don't like my narrative; you look almost sick—shall I defer the rest to another day?"

"No, sir, finish it now; I pity you—I do earnestly pity you. What did you do when you found she was mad?"

"Jane, I approached the verge of despair; a remnant of self respect was all that intervened between me and the gulf. In the eyes of the world, I was doubtless covered with dishonor; but I resolved to be clean in my own sight. Still, society associated my name and person with hers; I yet saw her and heard her daily. I knew that while she lived I could never be the husband of another and better wife; and, though five years my senior (her family and her father had lied to me even in the particular of her age), she was likely to live as long as I, being as robust in frame as she was infirm in mind. Thus, at the age of twenty-six, I was hopeless.

"One night I had been awakened by her yells—(since the medical men had pronounced her mad, she had, of course, been shut up)—it was a fiery West Indian night; one of the description that frequently precede the hurricanes of those climates. Being unable to sleep in bed, I got up and opened the window. The air was like sulfur steams—I could find no refreshment anywhere. Mosquitoes came buzzing in and hummed sullenly round the room; the sea, which I could hear from thence, rumbled dull like an earthquake—black clouds were casting up over it; the moon was setting in the waves, broad and red, like a hot cannon ball—she threw her last bloody glance over a world quivering with the ferment of tempest.

"I was physically influenced by the atmosphere and scene, and my ears were filled with the curses the maniac still shrieked out; wherein she momentarily mingled my name with such a tone of demon hate, with such language!—no professed harlot ever had a fouler vocabulary than she: though two rooms off, I heard every word—the thin partitions of the West India house opposing but slight obstruction to her wolfish cries.

"'This life is hell,' said I at last, 'this is the air—those are the sounds of the bottomless pit! I have a right to deliver myself from it if I can. Of the fanatic's burning eternity I have no fear: there is not a future state worse than this present one—let me break away, and go home to God!'

"I said this whilst I knelt down at, and unlocked a trunk which contained a brace of loaded pistols: I mean to shoot myself. I only entertained the intention for a moment; for, not being insane, the crisis of exquisite and unalloyed despair, which had originated the wish and design of self destruction, was past in a second.

"A wind fresh from Europe blew over the ocean and rushed through the open window: the storm broke, streamed, thundered, blazed, and the air grew pure.

I then framed and fixed a resolution. While I walked under the dripping orange trees of my wet garden, and amongst its drenched pomegranates and pineapples, and while the radiant dawn of the tropics kindled round me—I reasoned thus, Jane—and now listen; for it was true Wisdom that consoled me in that hour, and showed me the right path to follow.

"The sweet wind from Europe was still whispering in the refreshed leaves, and the Atlantic was thundering in glorious liberty; my heart, dried up and scorched for a long time. My being longed for renewal—my soul thirsted for a pure draught. I saw hope revive—and felt regeneration possible. From a flowery arch at the bottom of my garden I gazed over the sea—bluer than the sky: the old world was beyond; clear prospects opened thus –

"'Go,' said Hope, 'and live again in Europe: there it is not known what a sullied name you bear, nor what a filthy burden is bound to you. You may take the maniac with you to England; confine her with due attendance and precautions at Thornfield: then travel yourself to what clime you will, and form what new tie you like. That woman, who has so abused your long suffering, so sullied your name, so outraged your honor, so blighted your youth, is not your wife, nor are you her husband. See that she is cared for as her condition demands, and you have done all that God and humanity require of you. Let her identity, her connection with yourself, be buried in oblivion: you are bound to impart them to no living being. Place her in safety and comfort: shelter her degradation with secrecy, and leave her.'

"I acted precisely on this suggestion. My father and brother had not made my marriage known to their acquaintance; because, in the very first letter I wrote to apprise them of the union—having already begun to experience extreme disgust of its consequences, and, from the family character and constitution, seeing a hideous future opening to me—I added an urgent charge to keep it secret: and very soon the infamous conduct of the wife my father had selected for me was such as to make him blush to own her as his daughter-in-law. Far from desiring to publish the connection, he became as anxious to conceal it as myself.

"To England, then, I conveyed her; a fearful voyage I had with such a monster in the vessel. Glad was I when I at last got her to Thornfield, and saw her safely lodged in that third story room, of whose secret inner cabinet she has now for ten years made a wild beast's den—a goblin's cell. I had some trouble in finding an attendant for her, as it was necessary to select one on whose fidelity dependence could be placed; for her ravings would inevitably betray my secret:

besides, she had lucid intervals of days—sometimes weeks—which she filled up with abuse of me. At last I hired Grace Poole. She and the surgeon, Carter (who dressed Mason's wounds that night he was stabbed and worried), are the only two I have ever admitted to my confidence.

Mrs. Fairfax may indeed have suspected something, but she could have gained no precise knowledge as to facts. Grace has, on the whole, proved a good keeper; though, owing partly to a fault of her own, of which it appears nothing can cure her, and which is incident to her harassing profession, her vigilance has been more than once lulled and baffled. The lunatic is both cunning and malignant; she has never failed to take advantage of her guardian's temporary lapses; once to secret the knife with which she stabbed her brother, and twice to possess herself of the key of her cell, and issue therefrom in the night time. On the first of these occasions, she perpetrated the attempt to burn me in my bed; on the second, she paid that ghastly visit to you.

"I thank Providence, who watched over you, that she then spent her fury on your wedding apparel, which perhaps brought back vague reminiscences of her own bridal days: but on what might have happened, I cannot endure to reflect.

"And what, sir," I asked, while he paused, "did you do when you had settled her here? Where did you go?"

"What did I do, Jane? I transformed myself into a will-o'-the-wisp. Where did I go? I pursued wild wanderings. I sought the Continent, and went devious through all its lands. My fixed desire was to seek and find a good and intelligent woman, whom I could love: a contrast to the fury I left at Thornfield—"

"But you could not marry, sir."

"I had determined and was convinced that I could and ought. It was not my original intention to deceive, as I have deceived you. I meant to tell my tale plainly, and make my proposals openly: and it appeared to me so absolutely rational that I should be considered free to love and be loved, I never doubted some woman might be found willing and able to understand my case and accept me, in spite of the curse with which I was burdened."

"Well, sir? What next? How did you proceed? What came of such an event? Did you find any one you liked? Did you ask her to marry you? What did she say?"

"I can tell you whether I found any one I liked, and whether I asked her to marry me: but what she said is yet to be recorded in the book of Fate. For ten long years I roved about, living first in one capital, then another: sometimes in St. Petersburg; oftener in Paris; occasionally in Rome, Naples, and Florence. Provided with plenty of money and the passport of an old name, I could choose my own society: no circles were closed against me.

"I sought my ideal of a woman amongst English ladies, French countesses, Italian signoras, and German grafinnen. I could not find her. Sometimes, for a fleeting moment, I thought I caught a glance, heard a tone, beheld a form, which announced the realization of my dream: but I was presently undeserved.

"You are not to suppose that I desired perfection, either of mind or person. I longed only for what suited me—for the antipodes of the Creole: and I longed vainly. Amongst them all I found not one whom, had I been ever so free, I—warned as I was of the risks, the horrors, the loathings of incongruous unions—would have asked to marry me. Disappointment made me reckless. I tried dissipation—never debauchery: that I hated, and hate. Any enjoyment that bordered on riot seemed to approach me to my cursed wife, and I eschewed it.

"Yet I could not live alone; so I tried the companionship of mistresses. The first I chose was Celine Varens—another of those steps which make a man spurn himself when he recalls them. You already know what she was, and how my liaison with her terminated.

"She had two successors: an Italian, Giacinta, and a German, Clara; both considered singularly handsome. What was their beauty to me in a few weeks? Giacinta was unprincipled and violent: I tired of her in three months. Clara was honest and quiet; but heavy, mindless, and unimpressible: not one whit to my taste. I was glad to give her a sufficient sum to set her up in a good line of business, and so get decently rid of her. But, Jane, I see by your face you are not forming a very favorable opinion of me just now. You think me an unfeeling, loose principled rake: don't you?"

"I don't like you so well as I have done sometimes, indeed, sir. Did it not seem to you in the least wrong to live in that way, first with one mistress and then another? You talk of it as a mere matter of course."

"It was with me; and I did not like it. It was a grovelling fashion of existence: I should never like to return to it. Hiring a mistress is the next worse thing to buying a slave: both are often by nature, and always by position, inferior: and to live familiarly with inferiors is degrading. I now hate the recollection of the time I passed with Celine, Giacinta, and Clara."

I felt the truth of these words; and I drew from them the certain inference, that if I were so far to forget myself and all the teaching that had ever been instilled into me, as— under any pretext—with any justification—through any temptation—to become the successor of these poor girls, he would one day regard me with the same feeling which now in his mind desecrated their memory. I did not give utterance to this conviction: it was enough to feel it. I impressed it on my heart, that it might remain there to serve me as aid in the time of trial.

"Now, Jane, you are looking grave. You disapprove of me still, I see. But let me come to the point. Last January, rid of all mistresses—in a harsh, bitter frame of mind, the result of a useless, roving, lonely life— corroded with disappointment, sourly disposed against all men, and especially against all womankind (for I began to regard the notion of an intellectual, faithful, loving woman as a mere dream), recalled by business, I came back to England.

"On a frosty winter afternoon, I rode in sight of Thornfield Hall. Abhorred spot! I expected no peace—no pleasure there. Riding my horse in Hay Lane I saw a quiet little figure sitting by herself. I passed it as negligently as I did the willow tree opposite to it: I had no presentiment of what it would be to me; no inward warning that the arbitress of my life—my genius for good or evil—waited there in humble guise. I did not know it, even when, on the occasion of my horse's accident, it came up and gravely offered me help. Childish and slender creature! It seemed as if a linnet had hopped to my foot and proposed to bear me on its tiny wing. I was surly; but the thing would not go: it stood by me with strange perseverance, and looked and spoke with a sort of authority. I must be aided, and by that hand: and aided I was.

"When once I had pressed the frail shoulder, something new—a fresh sap and sense—stole into my frame. It was well I had learnt that this elf must return to me—that it belonged to my house down below or I could not have felt it pass away from under my hand, and seen it vanish behind the dim hedge, without singular regret. I heard you come home that night, Jane, though probably you were not aware that I thought of you or watched for you. The next day I observed you—myself unseen—for half an hour, while you played with Adele in the gallery.

"It was a snowy day, I recollect, and you could not go out of doors. I was in my room; the door was ajar: I could both listen and watch. Adele claimed your outward attention for a while; yet I fancied your thoughts were elsewhere: but you were very patient with her, my little Jane; you talked to her and amused her a long time. When at last she left you, you lapsed at once into deep reverie:

you betook yourself slowly to pace the gallery. Now and then, in passing a casement, you glanced out at the thick falling snow; you listened to the sobbing wind, and again you paced gently on and dreamed.

"I think those day visions were not dark: there was a pleasurable illumination in your eye occasionally, a soft excitement in your aspect, which told of no bitter, bilious, hypochondriac brooding: your look revealed rather the sweet musings of youth when its spirit follows on willing wings the flight of Hope up and on to an ideal heaven. The voice of Mrs. Fairfax, speaking to a servant in the hall, wakened you: and how curiously you smiled to and at yourself, Jane!

"There was much sense in your smile: it was very shrewd, and seemed to make light of your own abstraction. It seemed to say—"My fine visions are all very well, but I must not forget they are absolutely unreal. I have a rosy sky and a green flowery Eden in my brain; but without, I am perfectly aware, lies at my feet a rough tract to travel, and around me gather black tempests to encounter." You ran downstairs and demanded of Mrs. Fairfax some occupation: the weekly house accounts to make up, or something of that sort, I think it was. I was vexed with you for getting out of my sight.

"Impatiently I waited for evening, when I might summon you to my presence. An unusual—to me—a perfectly new character I suspected was yours: I desired to search it deeper and know it better. You entered the room with a look and air at once shy and independent: you were quaintly dressed—much as you are now. I made you talk: ere long I found you full of strange contrasts.

"Your garb and manner were restricted by rule; your air was often diffident, and altogether that of one refined by nature, but absolutely unused to society, and a good deal afraid of making herself disadvantageously conspicuous by some solecism or blunder; yet when addressed, you lifted a keen, a daring, and a glowing eye to your interlocutor's face: there was penetration and power in each glance you gave; when plied by close questions, you found ready and round answers.

"Very soon you seemed to get used to me: I believe you felt the existence of sympathy between you and your grim and cross master, Jane; for it was astonishing to see how quickly a certain pleasant ease tranquilized your manner: snarl as I would, you showed no surprise, fear, annoyance, or displeasure at my moroseness; you watched me, and now and then smiled at me with a simple yet sagacious grace I cannot describe. I was at once content and stimulated with what I saw: I liked what I had seen, and wished to see more.

"Yet, for a long time, I treated you distantly, and sought your company rarely. I was an intellectual epicure, and wished to prolong the gratification of making this novel and piquant acquaintance: besides, I was for a while troubled with a haunting fear that if I handled the flower freely its bloom would fade—the sweet charm of freshness would leave it. I did not then know that it was no transitory blossom, but rather the radiant resemblance of one, cut in an indestructible gem.

"Moreover, I wished to see whether you would seek me if I shunned you— but you did not; you kept in the schoolroom as still as your own desk and easel; if by chance I met you, you passed me as soon, and with as little token of recognition, as was consistent with respect. Your habitual expression in those days, Jane, was a thoughtful look; not despondent, for you were not sickly; but not buoyant, for you had little hope, and no actual pleasure. I wondered what you thought of me, or if you ever thought of me, and resolved to find this out.

"I resumed my notice of you. There was something glad in your glance, and genial in your manner, when you conversed: I saw you had a social heart; it was the silent schoolroom— it was the tedium of your life—that made you mournful. I permitted myself the delight of being kind to you; kindness stirred emotion soon: your face became soft in expression, your tones gentle; I liked my name pronounced by your lips in a grateful happy accent.

"I used to enjoy a chance meeting with you, Jane, at this time: there was a curious hesitation in your manner: you glanced at me with a slight troubled hovering doubt: you did not know what my caprice might be— whether I was going to play the master and be stern, or the friend and be benignant. I was now too fond of you often to simulate the first whim; and, when I stretched my hand out cordially, such bloom and light and bliss rose to your young, wistful features, I had much ado often to avoid straining you then and there to my heart."

"Don't talk any more of those days, sir," I interrupted, furtively dashing away some tears from my eyes; his language was torture to me; for I knew what I must do—and do soon—and all these reminiscences, and these revelations of his feelings only made my work more difficult.

"No, Jane," he returned: "what necessity is there to dwell on the Past, when the Present is so much surer—the Future so much brighter?"

I shuddered to hear the infatuated assertion. "You see now how the case stands—do you not?" he continued. "After a youth and manhood passed half in unutterable misery and half in dreary solitude, I have for the first time found what I can truly love—I have found you. You are my sympathy—my better self —my good angel. I am bound to you. I think you good, gifted, lovely: a fervent, a solemn passion is in my heart; it leans to you, draws you to me, wraps my existence about you, and, kindling in pure, powerful flame, fuses you and me in one.

"It was because I felt and knew this, that I resolved to marry you. To tell me that I had already a wife is empty mockery: you know now that I had but a hideous demon. I was wrong to attempt to deceive you; but I feared a stubbornness that exists in your character. I wanted to have you safe before hazarding confidences.

"This was cowardly: I should have appealed to your nobleness and magnanimity at first, as I do now—opened to you plainly my life of agony— described to you my hunger and thirst after a higher and worthier existence— shown to you, not my RESOLUTION, but my resistless BENT to love faithfully and well, where I am faithfully and well loved in return. Then I should have asked you to accept my pledge of fidelity and to give me yours. Jane—give it me now."

A pause. "Why are you silent, Jane?" I was experiencing an ordeal. A hand of fiery iron grasped me, a struggle of blackness and burning! Not a human being that ever lived could wish to be loved better than I was loved; and him who thus loved me I absolutely worshiped. I must renounce love and idol. One drear word comprised my intolerable duty—"Depart!"

"Jane, you understand what I want of you? Just this promise—"I will be yours, Mr. Rochester."

"Mr. Rochester, I will NOT be yours."

Another long silence.

"Jane!" recommenced he, with a gentleness that broke me down with grief, and turned me stone cold with ominous terror—for this still voice was the pant of a lion rising— "Jane, do you mean to go one way in the world, and to let me go another?"

"I do."

"Jane", bending towards and embracing me, "do you mean it now?"

"I do."

"And now?" softly kissing my forehead and cheek.

"I do," extricating myself from restraint rapidly and completely.

"Oh, Jane, this is bitter! This—this is wicked. It would not be wicked to love me."

"It would be wicked to obey you." A wild look raised his brows and crossed his features. I laid my hand on the back of a chair for support, I shook, I feared—but I resolved.

"One instant, Jane. Give one glance to my horrible life when you are gone. All happiness will be torn away with you. What then is left? For a wife I have but the maniac upstairs. What shall I do, Jane? Where turn for a companion and for some hope?"

"Do as I do: trust in God and yourself. Believe in heaven. Hope to meet again there."

"Then you will not yield?"

"No."

"Then you condemn me to live wretched and to die accursed?" His voice rose.

"I advise you to live sinless, and I wish you to die tranquil."

"Then you snatch love and innocence from me?"

"Mr. Rochester, I no more assign this fate to you than I grasp at it for myself. We were born to strive and endure— you as well as I: do so. You will forget me before I forget you."

"Is it better to drive a fellow creature to despair than to transgress a mere human law, no man being injured by the breach? for you have neither relatives nor acquaintances whom you need fear to offend by living with me?"

This was true: and while he spoke my very conscience and reason turned traitors against me, and charged me with crime in resisting him. They spoke almost as loud as Feeling: and that clamored wildly. "Oh, comply!" it said. "Think of his misery; think of his danger—look at his state when left alone; remember his headlong nature; consider the recklessness following on despair —soothe him; save him; love him; tell him you love him and will be his. Who in the world cares for YOU? or who will be injured by what you do?"

Still indomitable was the reply—"I care for myself. The more solitary, the more friendless, the more unsustained I am, the more I will respect myself. I will keep the law given by God; sanctioned by man. I will hold to those principles."

I retired to the door. "You are going, Jane?"

"I am going, sir."

"You are leaving me?"

"Yes."

"You will not come? You will not be my comforter, my rescuer? My deep love, my wild woe, my frantic prayer, are all nothing to you?"

What unutterable pathos was in his voice! How hard it was to state firmly, "I am going."

"Jane!"

"Mr. Rochester!"

"Withdraw, then,—I consent; but remember, you leave me here in anguish. Go up to your own room; think over all I have said, and, Jane, cast a glance on my sufferings—think of me."

He turned away; he threw himself on his face on the sofa. "Oh, Jane! my hope —my love—my life!" broke in anguish from his lips. Then came a deep, strong sob.

I had already gained the door; but, reader, I walked back—walked back as determinedly as I had retreated. I knelt down by him; I turned his face from the cushion to me; I kissed his cheek; I smoothed his hair with my hand.

"God bless you, my dear master!" I said. "God keep you from harm and wrong —direct you, solace you—reward you well for your past kindness to me."

"Little Jane's love would have been my best reward," he answered; "without it, my heart is broken. But Jane will give me her love: yes—nobly, generously."

Up the blood rushed to his face; forth flashed the fire from his eyes; erect he sprang; he held his arms out; but I evaded the embrace, and at once quitted the room.

"Farewell!" was the cry of my heart as I left him. Despair added, "Farewell forever!"

[[Realizing that her relationship with Mr. Rochester was impossible Jane fled. After wandering hungry and desperate Jane found a haven with two sisters and a brother, the Rivers family. The brother found Jane a position to teach at a charity school. An uncle of Jane's died and left her a large sum of money. Since Jane's uncle happened to also be the uncle of her new friends, Jane decided to split her inheritance equally with her three new found cousins.]]

[[The brother, St. John, planned to travel to India for missionary work. He implored Jane to marry him and accompany him. Jane was almost enticed but realized that the brother was seeking a helpmate and missionary partner rather than a soul embracing union.]]

[[Jane resided with the Rivers family for almost a year. One night after Jane had declined St. John marriage proposal, she heard Mr. Rochester calling her. Jane realized it was only Mr. Rochester whom she truly loved. She immediately set out for Thornfield. The mansion had burned to the ground. The fire had been set by Bertha Mason, Mr. Rochester's insane wife. She died. Mr. Rochester valiantly saved the servants. His injuries caused him to lose his eyesight and his left hand. Jane traveled to Mr. Rochester's new home.]]

"Give the tray to me; I will carry it to him." The tray shook as I held it; the water spilled from the glass; my heart struck my ribs loud and fast.

This parlor looked gloomy: a neglected fire burnt low in the grate; and, leaning over it, with his head supported against the high, old fashioned mantelpiece, appeared the blind tenant of the room. His old dog, Pilot, lay on one side. Pilot pricked up his ears, then jumped up with a yelp and a whine, and bounded towards me: he almost knocked the tray from my hands. I set it on the table; then patted him, and said softly, "Lie down!" Mr. Rochester turned mechanically to SEE what the commotion was: but as he saw nothing, he sighed.

"Give me the water, Mary," he said. I approached him. Pilot followed me, still excited.

"What is the matter?" he inquired. "Down, Pilot!" I again said. He checked the water on its way to his lips, and seemed to listen: he drank, and put the glass down. "This is you, Mary, is it not?"

"Mary is in the kitchen," I answered. He put out his hand with a quick gesture, but not seeing where I stood, he did not touch me. "Who is this? Who is this?" he demanded, trying, as it seemed, to SEE, and unavailing and distressing attempt! "Answer me—speak again!" he ordered, imperiously and aloud.

"Will you have a little more water, sir? I spilled half of what was in the glass," I said.

"WHO is it? WHAT is it? Who speaks?"

"Pilot knows me, and John and Mary know I am here. I came only this evening," I answered.

"Great God!—what delusion has come over me? What sweet madness has seized me?"

"No delusion—no madness: your mind, sir, is too strong for delusion."

"And where is the speaker? Is it only a voice? Oh! I CANNOT see, but I must feel, or my heart will stop and my brain burst. Whatever—whoever you are—be perceptible to the touch or I cannot live!"

He groped; I arrested his wandering hand, and held it in both mine.

"Her very fingers!" he cried; "her small, slight fingers! If so there must be more of her."

His muscular hand broke from my custody; my arm was seized, my shoulder—neck—waist—I was entwined and gathered to him.

"Is it Jane? WHAT is it? This is her shape—this is her size—"

"And this her voice," I added. "She is all here: her heart, too. God bless you, sir! I am glad to be so near you again."

"Jane Eyre!—Jane Eyre," was all he said. "My dear master," I answered, "I am Jane Eyre: I have found you out—I am come back to you."

"In truth?—in the flesh? My living Jane?"

"You touch me, sir,—you hold me, and fast enough: I am not vacant like air, am I?"

"My living darling! These are certainly her limbs, and these her features; but I cannot be so blest, after all my misery. It is a dream; such dreams as I have had at night when I have clasped her once more to my heart, as I do now; and kissed her, as thus—and felt that she loved me, and trusted that she would not leave me."

"Which I never will, sir, from this day."

"Never will, says the vision? But I always woke and found it an empty mockery; and I was desolate and abandoned—my life dark, lonely, hopeless—my soul athirst and forbidden to drink—my heart famished and never to be fed. Gentle, soft dream, nestling in my arms now, you will fly, too. Embrace me, Jane."

"There, sir—and there!" I pressed my lips to his once brilliant and now rayless eyes—I swept his hair from his brow, and kissed that too. He suddenly seemed to arouse himself: the conviction of the reality of all this seized him.

"It is you—is it, Jane? You are come back to me then?"

"I am."

"And you do not lie dead in some ditch under some stream? And you are not a pining outcast amongst strangers?"

"No, sir! I am an independent woman now."

"Independent! What do you mean, Jane?"

"My uncle in Madeira died, and he left me five thousand pounds."

"Ah! this is practical—this is real!" he cried: "I should never dream that. Besides, there is that peculiar voice of hers, so animating and piquant, as well as soft: it cheers my withered heart; it puts life into it.—What, Jane! Are you an independent woman? A rich woman?"

"If you won't let me live with you, I can build a house of my own close up to your door, and you may come and sit in my parlor when you want company of an evening."

"But as you are rich, Jane, you have now, no doubt, friends who will look after you, and not suffer you to devote yourself to a blind lameter like me?"

"I told you I am independent, sir, as well as rich: I am my own mistress."

"And you will stay with me?"

"Certainly—unless you object. I will be your neighbor, your nurse, your housekeeper. I find you lonely: I will be your companion—to read to you, to walk with you, to sit with you, to wait on you, to be eyes and hands to you. Cease to look so melancholy, my dear master; you shall not be left desolate, so long as I live."

He replied not: he seemed serious—abstracted; he sighed; he appeared about to speak: he closed them again. Perhaps I had too rashly over leaped conventionalities; and he, like St. John, saw impropriety in my inconsiderateness. I had indeed made my proposal from the idea that he wished and would ask me to be his wife: an expectation, not the less certain because unexpressed, had buoyed me up, that he would claim me at once as his own.

But no hint to that effect escaping him and his countenance becoming more overcast, I suddenly remembered that I might have been all wrong, and was perhaps playing the fool unwittingly; and I began gently to withdraw myself from his arms—but he eagerly snatched me closer.

"No—no—Jane; you must not go. No—I have touched you, heard you, felt the comfort of your presence—the sweetness of your consolation: I cannot give up these joys. I have little left in myself—I must have you. The world may laugh—may call me absurd, selfish—but it does not signify. My very soul demands you: it will be satisfied."

"Well, sir, I will stay with you: I have said so."

"Yes—but you understand one thing by staying with me; and I understand another. You, perhaps, could make up your mind to be about my hand and chair—to wait on me as a kind little nurse (for you have an affectionate heart and a generous spirit, which prompt you to make sacrifices for those you pity), and that ought to suffice for me no doubt. I suppose I should now entertain none but fatherly feelings for you: do you think so? Come—tell me."

"I will think what you like, sir: I am content to be only your nurse, if you think it better."

"But you cannot always be my nurse, Jane: you are young—you must marry one day."

"I don't care about being married."

"You should care, Jane: if I were what I once was, I would try to make you care —but—a sightless block!"

He relapsed again into gloom. I, on the contrary, became more cheerful, and took fresh courage: these last words gave me an insight as to where the difficulty lay; and as it was no difficulty with me, I resumed a livelier vein of conversation.

"It is time some one undertook to rehumanise you," said I, parting his thick and long uncut locks; "for I see you are being metamorphosed into a lion, or something of that sort. You have a "faux air" of Nebuchadnezzar in the fields about you, that is certain: your hair reminds me of eagles' feathers."

"On this arm, I have neither hand nor nails," he said, drawing the mutilated limb from his breast, and showing it to me. "It is a mere stump—a ghastly sight! Don't you think so, Jane?"

"It is a pity to see it; and a pity to see your eyes—and the scar of fire on your forehead: and the worst of it is, one is in danger of loving you too well for all this; and making too much of you."

"I thought you would be revolted, Jane, when you saw my arm, and my scared face."

"Did you? Don't tell me so—lest I should say something disparaging to your judgment. Now, let me leave you an instant, to make a better fire, and have the hearth swept up. Can you tell when there is a good fire?"

"Yes; with the right eye I see a glow—a ruddy haze."

"And you see the candles?"

"Very dimly—each is a luminous cloud."

"Can you see me?"

"No, my fairy: but I am only too thankful to hear and feel you."

"When do you take supper?"

"I never take supper."

"But you shall have some tonight. I am hungry: so are you, I daresay, only you forget."

My spirits were excited, and with pleasure and ease I talked to him during supper, and for a long time after. There was no harassing restraint, no repressing of glee and vivacity with him; for with him I was at perfect ease, because I knew I suited him; all I said or did seemed either to console or revive him. Delightful consciousness! It brought to life and light my whole nature: in his presence I thoroughly lived; and he lived in mine. Blind as he was, smiles and joy played over his face.

After supper, he began to ask me many questions, of where I had been, what I had been doing, how I had found him out; but I gave him only very partial replies: it was too late to enter into particulars that night. Besides, I wished to touch no deep thrilling chord—to open no fresh well of emotion in his heart: my sole present aim was to cheer him. Cheered, as I have said, he was: and yet but by fits. If a moment's silence broke the conversation, he would turn restless, touch me, then say, "Jane."

"You are altogether a human being, Jane? You are certain of that?"

"I conscientiously believe so, Mr. Rochester."

"Yet how, on this dark and doleful evening, could you so suddenly rise on my lone hearth? I stretched my hand to take a glass of water from a hireling, and it was given me by you: I asked a question, expecting John's wife to answer me, and your voice spoke at my ear."

"Because I had come in, in Mary's stead, with the tray."

"And there is enchantment in the very hour I am now spending with you. Who can tell what a dark, dreary, hopeless life I have dragged on for months past? Doing nothing, expecting nothing; merging night in day; feeling but the sensation of cold when I let the fire go out, of hunger when I forgot to eat: and then a ceaseless sorrow, and, at times, a very delirium of desire to behold my Jane again. Yes: for her restoration I longed, far more than for that of my lost sight.

"How can it be that Jane is with me, and says she loves me? Will she not depart as suddenly as she came? Tomorrow, I fear I shall find her no more."

A commonplace, practical reply, out of the train of his own disturbed ideas, was, I was sure, the best and most reassuring for him in this frame of mind.

"Where is the use of doing me good in any way, beneficent spirit, when, at some fatal moment, you will again desert me—passing like a shadow, whither and how to me unknown, and for me remaining afterwards undiscoverable?"

"Have you a comb, sir?"

"What for, Jane?"

"Just to comb out this shaggy black mane. I find you rather alarming, when I examine you close at hand."

"Am I hideous, Jane?"

"Very, sir: you always were, you know."

"The wickedness has not been taken out of you, wherever you have sojourned."

"Yet I have been with good people; far better than you: a hundred times better people; possessed of ideas and views you never entertained in your life: quite more refined and exalted."

"Who the deuce have you been with?"

"If you twist in that way you will make me pull the hair out of your head; and then I think you will cease to entertain doubts of my substantiality."

"Who have you been with, Jane?"

"You shall not get it out of me tonight, sir; you must wait till tomorrow; to leave my tale half told, will, you know, be a sort of security that I shall appear at your breakfast table to finish it. By-the-bye, I must mind not to rise on your hearth with only a glass of water then: I must bring an egg at the least, to say nothing of fried ham."

"You mocking changeling—fairy born and human bred! You make me feel as I have not felt these twelve months. If Saul could have had you for his David, the evil spirit would have been exorcised without the aid of the harp."

"There, sir, you are redd up and made decent. Now I'll leave you: I have been traveling these last three days, and I believe I am tired. Good night."

"Just one word, Jane: were there only ladies in the house where you have been?"

I laughed and made my escape, still laughing as I ran upstairs. "A good idea!" I thought with glee. "I see I have the means of fretting him out of his melancholy for some time to come."

Very early the next morning I heard him up and astir, wandering from one room to another. As soon as Mary came down I heard the question: "Is Miss Eyre here?" Then: "Which room did you put her into? Was it dry? Is she up? Go and ask if she wants anything; and when she will come down."

I came down early for breakfast. Entering the room very softly, I had a view of him before he discovered my presence. It was mournful. I had meant to be gay and careless, but the powerlessness of the strong man touched my heart to the quick.

"It is a bright, sunny morning, sir," I said. "The rain is over and gone, and there is a tender shining after it: you shall have a walk soon."

I had wakened the glow: his features beamed. "Oh, you are indeed there, my skylark! Come to me. You are not gone: not vanished? All the sunshine I can feel is in your presence."

Tears gathered in my eyes to hear this avowal of his dependence. I brushed them away and busied myself with preparing breakfast.

Most of the morning was spent in the open air. I led him out of the wet and wild wood into some cheerful fields: I described to him how brilliantly green they were; how the flowers and hedges looked refreshed; how sparklingly blue was the sky. I sought a seat for him in a hidden and lovely spot; nor did I refuse to let him, when seated, place me on his knee. Why should I, when both he and I were happier near than apart? Pilot lay beside us: all was quiet. He broke out suddenly while clasping me in his arms—

"Cruel, cruel deserter! Oh, Jane, what did I feel when I discovered you had fled, and when I could nowhere find you; and, after examining your apartment, ascertained that you had taken no money, nor anything which could serve as an equivalent! A pearl necklace I had given you lay untouched; your trunks were left corded and locked as they had been prepared for the bridal tour. What could my darling do, I asked, left destitute and penniless? And what did she do? Let me hear now."

Thus urged, I began the narrative of my experience for the last year. I softened considerably what related to the three days of wandering and starvation, because to have told him all would have been to inflict unnecessary pain: the little I did say lacerated his faithful heart deeper than I wished.

I should not have left him thus, he said, without any means of making my way: I should have told him my intention. I should have confided in him: he would never have forced me to be his mistress. He loved me far too well and too tenderly to constitute himself my tyrant: he would have given me half his fortune, without demanding so much as a kiss in return, rather than I should have flung myself friendless on the wide world. I had endured, he was certain, more than I had confessed to him.

"Well, whatever my sufferings had been, they were very short," I answered: and then I proceeded to tell him how I had been received at Moor House; how I had obtained the office of schoolmistress, etc. The accession of fortune, the discovery of my relations, followed in due order. Of course, St. John Rivers' name came in frequently in the progress of my tale. When I had done, that name was immediately taken up.

"This St. John, then, is your cousin?"

"Yes."

"You have spoken of him often: do you like him?"

"He was a very good man, sir; I could not help liking him."

"A good man. Does that mean a respectable well conducted man of fifty? Or what does it mean?"

"St John was only twenty-nine, sir."

"Is he a person of low stature, phlegmatic, and plain. A person whose goodness consists rather in his guiltlessness of vice, than in his prowess in virtue."

"He is untiringly active. Great and exalted deeds are what he lives to perform."

"But his brain? That is probably rather soft? He means well: but you shrug your shoulders to hear him talk?"

"He talks little, sir: what he does say is ever to the point. His brain is first rate, I should think not impressible, but vigorous."

"Is he an able man, then?"

"Truly able."

"A thoroughly educated man?"

"St. John is an accomplished and profound scholar."

"His manners, I think, you said are not to your taste?— priggish and parsonic?"

"I never mentioned his manners; but, unless I had a very bad taste, they must suit it; they are polished, calm, and gentlemanlike."

"His appearance,—I forget what description you gave of his appearance;—a sort of raw curate, half strangled with his white neckcloth, eh?"

"St. John dresses well. He is a handsome man: tall, fair, with blue eyes, and a Grecian profile."

(Aside.) "Damn him!"—(To me.) "Did you like him, Jane?"

"Yes, Mr. Rochester, I liked him: but you asked me that before."

I perceived, of course, the drift of my interlocutor. Jealousy had got hold of him: she stung him; but the sting was salutary: it gave him respite from the gnawing fang of melancholy. I would not, therefore, immediately charm the snake.

"Perhaps you would rather not sit any longer on my knee, Miss Eyre?" was the next somewhat unexpected observation.

"Why not, Mr. Rochester?"

"The picture you have just drawn is suggestive of a rather too overwhelming contrast. Your words have delineated very prettily a graceful Apollo: he is present to your imagination,—tall, fair, blue eyed, and with a Grecian profile. Your eyes dwell on a Vulcan,—a real blacksmith, brown, broad shouldered: and blind and lame into the bargain."

"I never thought of it, before; but you certainly are rather like Vulcan, sir."

"Well, you can leave me, ma"am: but before you go" (and he retained me by a firmer grasp than ever), "you will be pleased just to answer me a question or two." He paused.

"What questions, Mr. Rochester?" Then followed this cross examination. "St. John made you schoolmistress of Morton before he knew you were his cousin?"

"Yes."

"You would often see him? He would visit the school sometimes?"

"Daily."

"He would approve of your plans, Jane? I know they would be clever, for you are a talented creature!"

"He approved of them—yes."

"He would discover many things in you he could not have expected to find? Some of your accomplishments are not ordinary."

"I don't know about that."

"You had a little cottage near the school, you say: did he ever come there to see you?"

"Now and then?"

"Of an evening?"

"Once or twice." A pause. "How long did you reside with him and his sisters after the cousinship was discovered?"

"Five months."

"Did Rivers spend much time with the ladies of his family?"

"Yes; the back parlor was both his study and ours: he sat near the window, and we by the table."

"Did he study much?"

"A good deal."

"What? Hindostanee."

"And what did you do meantime?"

"I learnt German, at first."

"Did he teach you?"

"He did not understand German."

"Did he teach you nothing?"

"A little Hindostanee."

"Rivers taught you Hindostanee?"

"Yes, sir."

"And his sisters also?"

"No."

"Only you?"

"Only me."

"Did you ask to learn?"

"No."

"He wished to teach you?"

"Yes." A second pause. "Why did he wish it? Of what use could Hindostanee be to you?"

"He intended me to go with him to India."

"Ah! here I reach the root of the matter. He wanted you to marry him?"

"He asked me to marry him."

"That is a fiction—an impudent invention to vex me."

"I beg your pardon, it is the literal truth: he asked me more than once, and was as stiff about urging his point as ever you could be."

"Miss Eyre, I repeat it, you can leave me. How often am I to say the same thing?

Why do you remain pertinaciously perched on my knee, when I have given you notice to quit?"

"Because I am comfortable there."

"No, Jane, you are not comfortable there, because your heart is not with me: it is with this cousin—this St. John. Oh, till this moment, I thought my little Jane was all mine! I had a belief she loved me even when she left me: that was an atom of sweet in much bitter. Long as we have been parted, hot tears as I have wept over our separation, I never thought that while I was mourning her, she was loving another! But it is useless grieving. Jane, leave me: go and marry Rivers."

"Shake me off, then, sir,—push me away, for I'll not leave you of my own accord."

"Jane, I ever like your tone of voice: it still renews hope, it sounds so truthful. When I hear it, it carries me back a year. I forget that you have formed a new tie. But I am not a fool—go—"

"Where must I go, sir?"

"Your own way—with the husband you have chosen."

"Who is that?"

"You know—this St. John Rivers."

"He is not my husband, nor ever will be. He does not love me: I do not love him. He loves (as he CAN love, and that is not as you love) a beautiful young lady called Rosamond. He wanted to marry me only because he thought I should make a suitable missionary's wife, which she would not have done. He is and great, but severe; and, for me, cold as an iceberg. He is not like you, sir: I am not happy at his side, nor near him, nor with him. He has no indulgence for me —no fondness. He sees nothing attractive in me; not even youth—only a few useful mental points.—Then I must leave you, sir, to go to him?"

I shuddered involuntarily, and clung instinctively closer to my blind but beloved master. He smiled.

"What, Jane! Is this true? Is such really the state of matters between you and Rivers?"

"Absolutely, sir! Oh, you need not be jealous! I wanted to tease you a little to make you less sad: I thought anger would be better than grief. But if you wish me to love you, could you but see how much I DO love you, you would be content. All my heart is yours, sir: it belongs completely to you; and with you it would remain, even if fate were to exile me from your presence forever."

Again, as he kissed me, painful thoughts darkened his aspect. "My blindness! My crippled strength!" he murmured regretfully.

I caressed, in order to soothe him. I knew of what he was thinking, and wanted to speak for him, but dared not. As he turned aside his face a minute, I saw a tear slide from under the sealed eyelid, and trickle down the manly cheek. My heart swelled.

"I am no better than the old lightning struck chestnut tree in Thornfield orchard," he remarked. "And what right would that ruin have to bid a budding woodbine cover its decay with freshness?"

"You are no ruin, sir—no lightning struck tree: you are green and vigorous. Plants will grow about your roots, whether you ask them or not, because they take delight in your bountiful shadow; and as they grow they will lean towards you, and wind round you."

Again he smiled: I gave him comfort. "You speak of friends, Jane?" he asked. "Yes, of friends," I answered rather hesitatingly: for I knew I meant more than friends, but could not think of what other word to use. He helped me. "Ah! Jane. But I want a wife."

"Do you, sir?"

"Yes: is it news to you?"

"Of course: you said nothing about it before."

"Is it unwelcome news?"

"That depends on circumstances, sir—on your choice."

"Which you shall make for me, Jane. I will abide by your decision."

"Choose then, sir—HER WHO LOVES YOU BEST."

"I will at least choose—HER I LOVE BEST. Jane, will you marry me?"

"Yes, sir."

"A poor blind man, whom you will have to lead about by the hand?"

"Yes, sir."

"A crippled man, twenty years older than you, whom you will have to wait on?"

"Yes, sir."

"Truly, Jane?"

"Most truly, sir."

"Oh! my darling! God bless you and reward you!"

"Mr. Rochester, if ever I did a good deed in my life—if ever I thought a good thought—if ever I prayed a sincere and blameless prayer—if ever I wished a righteous wish,—I am rewarded now. To be your wife is, for me, to be as happy as I can be on earth."

"Because you delight in sacrifice."

"Sacrifice! What do I sacrifice? Famine for food, expectation for content. To be privileged to put my arms round what I value—to press my lips to what I love—to repose on what I trust: is that to make a sacrifice? If so, then certainly I delight in sacrifice."

"And to bear with my infirmities, Jane: to overlook my deficiencies."

"Which are none, sir, to me. I love you better now, when I can really be useful to you, than I did in your state of proud independence, when you disdained every part but that of the giver and protector."

"Hitherto I have hated to be helped—to be led: henceforth, I feel I shall hate it no more. I did not like to put my hand into a hireling's, but it is pleasant to feel it circled by Jane's little fingers. I preferred utter loneliness to the constant attendance of servants; but Jane's soft ministry will be a perpetual joy. Jane suits me: do I suit her?"

"To the finest fiber of my nature, sir."

"The case being so, we have nothing in the world to wait for: we must be married instantly."

He looked and spoke with eagerness: his old impetuosity was rising.

"We must become one flesh without any delay, Jane: there is but the license to get—then we marry."

"Mr. Rochester, I have just discovered the sun is far declined from its meridian, and Pilot is actually gone home to his dinner. Let me look at your watch."

"Jane, keep it henceforward: I have no use for it."

"It is nearly four o"clock in the afternoon, sir. Don't you feel hungry?"

"The third day from this must be our wedding day, Jane. Never mind fine clothes and jewels, now: all that is not worth a fillip."

"The sun has dried up all the rain drops, sir. The breeze is still: it is quite hot."

"We will go home through the wood: that will be the shadiest way."

He pursued his own thoughts without heeding me.

"Jane! you think me, I daresay, an irreligious dog: but my heart swells with gratitude to the beneficent God of this earth just now. He sees not as man sees, but far clearer: judges not as man judges, but far more wisely. I did wrong: I would have sullied my innocent flower—breathed guilt on its purity: the Omnipotent snatched it from me.

"I, in my stiff necked rebellion, almost cursed the dispensation: instead of bending to the decree, I defied it. Divine justice pursued its course; disasters came thick on me: I was forced to pass through the valley of the shadow of death.

"His chastisements are mighty; and one smote me which has humbled me forever. You know I was proud of my strength: but what is it now, when I must give it over to foreign guidance, as a child does its weakness? Of late, Jane—only—only of late—I began to see and acknowledge the hand of God in my doom. I began to experience remorse, repentance; the wish for reconcilement to my Maker. I began sometimes to pray: very brief prayers they were, but very sincere.

"Some days since: nay, I can number them—four; it was last Monday night, a singular mood came over me: one in which grief replaced frenzy—sorrow, sullenness. I had long had the impression that since I could nowhere find you, you must be dead. Late that night— perhaps it might be between eleven and twelve o"clock—ere I retired to my dreary rest, I supplicated God, that, if it seemed good to Him, I might soon be taken from this life, and admitted to that world to come, where there was still hope of rejoining Jane.

"I was in my own room, and sitting by the window, which was open: it soothed me to feel the balmy night air; though I could see no stars and only by a vague, luminous haze, knew the presence of a moon. I longed for thee, Jane! Oh, I longed for thee both with soul and flesh! I asked of God, at once in anguish and humility, if I had not been long enough desolate, afflicted, tormented; and might not soon taste bliss and peace once more. That I merited all I endured, I acknowledged—that I could scarcely endure more, I pleaded; and the alpha and omega of my heart's wishes broke involuntarily from my lips in the words

—"Jane! Jane! Jane!"

"Did you speak these words aloud?"

"I did, Jane. If any listener had heard me, he would have thought me mad: I pronounced them with such frantic energy."

"And it was last Monday night, somewhere near midnight?"

"Yes; but the time is of no consequence: what followed is the strange point. You will think me superstitious,—some superstition I have in my blood, and always had: nevertheless, this is true— true at least it is that I heard what I now relate.

"As I exclaimed "Jane! Jane! Jane!" a voice—I cannot tell whence the voice came, but I know whose voice it was—replied, "I am coming: wait for me;" and a moment after, went whispering on the wind the words—"Where are you?"

"I'll tell you, if I can, the idea, the picture these words opened to my mind. Where are you?" seemed spoken amongst mountains. I could have deemed that in some wild, lone scene, I and Jane were meeting. In spirit, I believe we must have met. You no doubt were, at that hour, in unconscious sleep, Jane: perhaps your soul wandered from its cell to comfort mine; for those were your accents as certain as I live—they were yours!"

Reader, it was on Monday night—near midnight—that I too had received the mysterious summons: those were the very words by which I replied to it. I listened to Mr. Rochester's narrative, but made no disclosure in return. If I told anything, my tale would be such as must necessarily make a profound impression on the mind of my hearer. Sufferings too prone to gloom, need not the deeper shade of the supernatural. I kept these things then, and pondered them in my heart.

"You cannot now wonder," continued my master, "that when you rose upon me so unexpectedly last night, I had difficulty in believing you any other than a mere voice and vision, something that would melt to silence and annihilation, as the midnight whisper and mountain echo had melted before. Now, I thank God! I know it to be otherwise. Yes, I thank God!"

He put me off his knee, rose, and reverently lifting his hat from his brow, and bending his sightless eyes to the earth, he stood in mute devotion. Only the last words of the worship were audible.

"I thank my Maker, that, in the midst of judgment, he has remembered mercy. I humbly entreat my Redeemer to give me strength to lead henceforth a purer life than I have done hitherto!"

Then he stretched his hand out to be led. I took that dear hand, held it a moment to my lips, then let it pass round my shoulder: being so much lower of stature than he, I served both for his prop and guide. We entered the wood, and wended homeward.

Reader, I married him. A quiet wedding we had: he and I, the parson and clerk, were alone present.

You have not quite forgotten Adele, have you, reader? I found in her a pleasing and obliging companion: docile, good tempered, and well principled. By her grateful attention to me and mine, she has long since well repaid any little kindness I ever had it in my power to offer her.

My tale draws to its close. I have now been married ten years. I know what it is to live entirely for and with what I love best on earth. I hold myself supremely blest—blest beyond what language can express; because I am my husband's life as fully is he is mine. No woman was ever nearer to her mate than I am: ever more absolutely bone of his bone and flesh of his flesh.

I know no weariness of my Edward's society: he knows none of mine, any more than we each do of the pulsation of our hearts. To be together is for us to be at once as free as in solitude, as gay as in company. We talk, I believe, all day long: to talk to each other is but a more animated and an audible thinking. All my confidence is bestowed on him, all his confidence is devoted to me; we are precisely suited in character—perfect concord is the result.

Mr. Rochester continued blind the first two years of our union. He eventually recovered the sight of that one eye. He cannot now see very distinctly: he cannot read or write much; but he can find his way without being led by the hand: the sky is no longer a blank to him—the earth no longer a void.

When his first born was put into his arms, he could see that the boy had inherited his own eyes, as they once were—large, brilliant, and black. On that occasion, he again, with a full heart, acknowledged that God had tempered judgment with mercy.

My Edward and I, then, are happy...